Edward Capern

Sungleams and Shadows

ISBN/EAN: 9783744742696

Printed in Europe, USA, Canada, Australia, Japan

Cover: Foto ©Andreas Hilbeck / pixelio.de

More available books at **www.hansebooks.com**

SUNGLEAMS AND SHADOWS

BY

EDWARD CAPERN,

AUTHOR OF "POEMS," "BALLADS AND SONGS," "WAYSIDE WARBLES,"
AND THE "DEVONSHIRE MELODIST."

Hark! Hey away! his "Lillelu,"
The throstle-cock is sounding;
It's O! to brush the bonny dew,
Where merry stags are bounding.
PAGE 77.

LONDON:
KENT & CO., PATERNOSTER ROW.

BIRMINGHAM:
CORNISH BROS., 37, NEW STREET.
HOUGHTON & HAMMOND, SCOTLAND PASSAGE.

1881.

Edward Capern

Sungleams and Shadows

"The murkiest wave hath its eddy of light,
    'The sunniest ripple its shade."

[Entered at Stationers' Hall.]

HOUGHTON AND HAMMOND, PRINTERS, BIRMINGHAM.

THIS VOLUME

IS DEDICATED, BY PERMISSION,

TO

ALDERMAN THÓMAS AVERY, J.P.,

EDGBASTON,

AS A MARK OF THE AUTHOR'S HIGH APPRECIATION

OF HIS

UNFAILING COURTESY,

AND THE

WARM INTEREST

HE HAS ALWAYS MANIFESTED

IN THE

SOCIAL, INTELLECTUAL AND MORAL ADVANCEMENT

OF

THE PEOPLE.

PREFACE.

THE second edition of "WAYSIDE WARBLES" being out of print, I have been repeatedly asked, either to re-publish them, or give the public a new volume of my lyrics. After duly considering the matter I have decided on adopting the latter course, and I trust that the contents of the present work will be found worthy of the same favour so generously accorded to my former productions.

As heretofore, I have sought my inspiration in the field and the lane, in the woodland and by the stream, and the majority of the poems now presented to the world for the first time, have been composed during my rambles.

I must not omit here to mention the obligations I owe to the Press for the very flattering manner in which it has always noticed my writings; and my best thanks and acknowledgments are also due to Mr. Thomas Murby, of 32, Bouverie Street, London, and the Proprietors of the *Gentleman's Magazine*, *Good Words*, *Saturday Journal*, *Day of*

Rest, *Mid-England*, *Leisure Hour*, *Fun*, *Hood's Comic Annual*, etc., etc., for their kindness in permitting me to use the Poems which had previously appeared in their publications.

It is right, too, that I should state for the information of my numerous friends, who were so good as to favour me with their support, when more than twelve months ago I first advertised "SUNGLEAMS AND SHADOWS," that, but for a severe and prolonged domestic affliction, this volume would have appeared at a much earlier date.

In conclusion, let me say I am deeply sensible of the fact that after being before the Public for a quarter of a century, I have, in addition to those of my old friends still surviving in Devon and elsewhere, whose interest in my work has never flagged from the commencement of my literary career, a large and increasing circle of readers in the Midlands, where I have resided during the past fourteen years, to all of whom I tender my most cordial and grateful thanks.

EDWARD CAPERN.

Heath Road, Harborne,
March 2nd, 1881.

CONTENTS.

SUNGLEAMS.

CONTENTS. ix.

SHADOWS.

LAYS FOR THE LITTLE ONES.

PATRIOTIC AND OTHER POEMS.

ERRATA.

Page 142, line 11, *for* " take Thee at," **read** " rest upon."
Page 168 (foot note), *for* " Church, &c.," *read* " In the Church, &c."
Page 177, line 12, *for* " angel's," *read* " angels'."
Page 185, line 17, *for* " excelleth," *read* " excellest."
Page 187 (foot note), *for* "Aug 9th," **read** "Aug. 9th, 1877,"
Page 123, *for* " borne," *read* " born."

SUNGLEAMS.

"The merry sunshine makes for earth
A happy holiday ;
And he who sings of Nature's mirth
Gives life a golden ray."

How sweet it is, when **mother Fancy rocks**
The wayward brain, **to saunter through a wood !**
An old place, full of many a lovely brood,
Tall **trees, green** arbours, and ground flowers in flocks.

WORDSWORTH.

TO THE READER.

SUN-GLEAMS and shadows? yes, just so ;
    Bright glintings of the May ;
And little palls on frozen snow,
    Beneath a cypress-spray.

Still, read no more, if thou would'st crave
    All sunshine, and no shade ;
While primrose makes her dewy grave
    Within her native glade.

Yet know, I almost worship light,
    And sometimes, thinking wrong,
Wish we had little less of night,
    And for the sigh, a song.

But, gentle reader, take my book
    As young men take their loves,
Away unto some quiet nook
    Made musical with doves ;

And having scanned it, pardon me
    For taxing so thy time,
Unless thine eye arrested be
    To revel in a rhyme.

Or thou hast learnt, with me, to sing
    Of simple wayside weeds—
To the wild music of the spring,
    That purls amid the reeds ;

And shout, as comes the bright bluebell,
    Delighted as a boy,
" I never can refuse to tell
    The world what I enjoy."

————

THE SECRET OF MY ART.

WHAT is the secret of my Art ?
    In honest faith I never knew it :
I simply play the loyal part,
    And write as nature bids me do it.

And oh ! of all the joys I know,
    There are but few like that of singing,
When souls with rapture overflow
    To fairy-love bells sweetly ringing ;

Most happy then it is for me,
    If I am in some ferny dingle,
And wandering, like a honey-bee,
    To the wild music of my jingle.

I have no other Art but this,
    I fly the fog, where fancy lingers,
And numbers, that will run amiss,
    Like those men count upon the fingers.

Right helter skelter on I dash,
    Unweeting of the tune or measure,
Delighted, with each sunny flash
    Of thought, alive with heart and pleasure.

And this would be reward enough,
    If self-enjoyment were the reason
That made me sing, by brake and bluff,
    The first fair floweret of each season:

But, when I find my artless songs
    Can make e'en chilly winter warmer,
And touch to mirth the children's tongues,
    Ambition makes me play the charmer.

PASTORAL PICTURES.

Twirling into quaintest notes
    Of interrogation,
As a host of feathered throats
    Sing with emulation ;
Mark the little lambs at play,
    Dancing to their praises,
Asking, in their pretty way,
    Where can be the daisies ?

Now athwart the azure sky,
    Paying spring a favour,
Shoots the gladsome lark on high,
    Music's living quaver ;—
Lilting up his airy way,
    Full of adoration ;—
Happy seraph of the May !
    For the new creation.

Daisies, rathe and rosy-rimm'd,
    'Mid the tender grasses,
Golden boss'd, and nectar brimm'd,
    Welcome now the lasses ;—
While around, from sea to sea,
    Mellow cuckoos singing,
Come to keep us company,
    Joyful tidings bringing.

Sweet, oh ! **sweet is summer-time,**
  White with hawthorn-blossoms,
Life's delight, and golden **prime**
  Of impassion'd bosoms.
When, from silv'ry clouds above,
  Down to marish rushes,
Nature chants one song of love,
  Choruss'd by the thrushes.

1879.

LILLELU.

ON HEARING THE THRUSH SING HIS FIRST SPRING SONG.

" LILLELU !" that's he I know,
  Listen, **love, he'll sing again,**
" Tewteweet, teweet, tewoo."
  What a charm is in his strain !
This is what he seems to say—
  " Winter ! thou hast had thy share,
Let our little maiden fair,
Snowdrop, show her face to-day,
  " Lillelu ! Lillelu ! Lillelu !"

"Lillelu!" that is the word
    The throstle trills when deep in love,
As, perched above his mate, the bird
    In tenderness outvies the dove :—
It means, if I interpret right,
    " My love is sweet, and she is near,
    The sweetest sweetling, is my dear ; "
And this he sings from morn to night—
    " Lillelu ! Lillelu ! Lillelu ! "

" Lillelu ! " just mark **the notes,**
    The cream and honey **of his song** ;
And **as the** strain mellifluous floats,
    And sweeps the fragrant vales along,
I catch, as I have caught, the soul
    Of everything he sings, and sense :—
    As hidden **by some hawthorn-fence,**
I've heard his bursts of passion roll,
    " Lillelu ! Lillelu ! Lillelu ! "

" Lillelu ! " the master-tone
    And key-note of each merry lay ;
For sings he not one song alone,
    He has a song for every day ;
And rich and various as his themes,
    So are the solos of his choice ;
    And given with a flexile voice,
In matins, and in vesper hymns,—
    " Lillelu ! Lillelu ! Lillelu ? "

"Lillelu!" the country side
　　Rings ever with the sweet refrain;
But would'st thou hear him in his pride,
　　Then seat thyself in yonder plain,
And **see** that he's a six-year-old,
　　A bird of courage in his prime,
　　And let young April be the time,
And thou shalt find him brave and **bold**—-
　　"Lillelu! Lillelu! Lillelu!"

"Lillelu!" he giveth thrice,
　　In the sweetest tone he sings,
"Toot-toot-toot," and "tulu" twice,
　　Till the whole theatre rings.
Then he makes his glorious runs
　　O'er the octaves to the close,
Major notes and minor ones,
　　Seeking, not till night, repose--
　　"Lillelu! Lillelu! Lillelu!"

February 10th, **1876**.

———

WOMAN.

Sweet woman brightens **daily life**,
　　By love and cheerful duty;
Our rainbow, in its storm of strife,
　　That paints the cloud with beauty.

A LOVE SONG.

A RAPTURE trilling from the heart,
    A gush of inspiration,
A sigh we breathe, when far apart,
    With musical vibration.

A thread, on which the poet strings
    The jewels of affection ;
A melody, the whole world sings,
    When Love makes his selection.

Who will may make the laws for me,
    Who will may build the city,
And pen the prosy things that be,
    Let me but pipe my ditty.

Some tender love-lay, nothing else,
    The simple song revealing ;
A power that stirs the vital pulse
    Of universal feeling.

Harborne, October 25th, 1876.

PURPOSE.

THUS a minstrel, as he ponder'd,
  Sang of purpose on a day,
As he saw men faint and falter
  At the dangers of the way.

" What is evil?   Who will answer?
  There is little we can find
That may not be made a blessing,
  As a buttress for the mind.

As the prospect wider opens
  To the climber in his path,
And the mower scents the fragrance
  Of his labour in the swath,

And the earth-root of the seedling
  Striketh down into the night,
While the blade, with soul diviner,
  Struggles upward to the light,

'Till the patience of the sower
  By the yellow sheaf is crown'd ;
So, in bitter pain and travail,
  Golden guerdons aye are found.

Up, my soul, then, and the hero
   Play **with** all thy might and main,
And, with trusty sword, advancing,
   Meet the battle thou would'st gain.

Who is he that dares to hinder
   Courage on a purpose bent?
Bid him stay the whizzing arrow
   By the master-archer sent;

Bid him bind the winds of Heaven,
   Still the tempest, **span** the sky,
Chain the comet, tame the ocean,
   Bar the lightnings as they fly.

Where's the rock too hard for boring
   When a diamond cuts the **way**?
And an earnest soul **in** action
   Is a fate the Gods obey.

What is hindrance to the lesser,
   To the greater is an aid.
Is the torrent by **a** boulder
   In its raging **fury** stay'd?

Opposition maketh valiant,
   And those mightiest are hail'd
Who with few in number triumph
   When by 'whelming **hosts** assail'd.

Throw the **coward down**, he flattens,
  Like **a soulless lump of lead** ;
But, the heavier falls the **hero**,
  Higher bounds he o'er your **head**.

Nothing that can be accomplish'd
  Is impossible to him ;
Clear he sees in cloudy regions
  Where the craven's sight is dim.

What's the Materhorn or Maëlstrom
  To the man with **soul to dare**,
Whose march-word, " **Nil** desperandum,"
  Cows the very fiend Despair ?

Naught **to him** are plotting mortals,
  As they **fret**, and fume, **and mar** ;
And, with petty hate and **envy**,
  Wound and harrass **in the war.**

Till a moth, then, stops the fountain,
  And a rushlight shames **the sun**,
And the mouse o'erturns **the mountain**,
  High **Resolve** his course **will run**,—

With a fixed and noble PURPOSE,
  Shouting, ' Death or Victory !
Man is not a two-legg'd creature,
  But a demi-god **is** he.' "

TO A MOSS ROSE.

Bright offspring of a fairy clime !
Embalmed in many an olden rhyme ;
When first we met, at summer time,
    In my belovèd West,—
Young Poesy came every day,
With song of bird, and bloomy spray,
    And all the world was blest.

A deeper blush suffused thy cheek,
Methought, when I essayed to speak
A word of praise, but words were **weak**
    To sing thy matchless worth ;
And yet at times my simple strains
Were honoured, for the singer's pains,
    Queen Rose of all the earth !

So dainty, and so delicate,
And so ethereal's thy state,
Young Zephyr wooed thee for his mate,
    With aromatic kiss ;
And wrapped thee in a robe of moss,
Lest Beauty's self should suffer loss,
    And life its rapture **miss.**

Enough! had I a golden flute,
Soft toned as is an elfin lute,
Thy meetest praise were worship mute,
　　While music filled the air
With melodies of birds and bees,
And whisperings of summer trees,
　　Sweet wonder of the fair !

August 1st, 1878.

MUTE-MELODY.

There is a silent music of the soul,
　That, waiting for an utterance in words,
Will burst at length, impatient of control,
　Like vernal melodies of singing birds.

OLD LOVE LANE.

Just a blue-bell, here and there, now marks the pleasant
　　way we took
To the cottage in the valley, by the little purling brook ;
There were balmy hawthorn hedgerows, then, with
　　primroses and fern,
And the red rose-campion met us, in the lane at
　　every turn.

In the merry month of April, when the willows **woo**
    the gale,
And miles of meadow-buttercups make golden every
    vale ;
And in the bonny May-moon time, when **daisies, all**
    aglow,
Paint every pleasant field with sweet white **showers**
    of sunny **snow.**

There we, halting, plucked the wilding, **and, a moment**
    to beguile,
Enquired of it our fortune, as we rested on the stile ;
But no vestige of the bankside lingers now, or gate, to
    show
The track of the old vanished lane of love's sweet
    long ago.

Edgbaston, **May, 1878.**

A WEDDING FAVOUR.

Love-wedded in these sunny times
    Of lily-bloom and rose,
Made sweeter with the scent of limes
    By every wind that blows ;
  Ye have a fragrant prophecy,
  And pledge, of rare felicity.

LOVE OF NATURE

EARTH seems pausing in her race ;—
  While the winds, I know not why,
Through the silent realms of space,
  Half-regretful softly sigh.

Yet the folk move to and fro,
  One may note them every day ;
Hasting come, and hasting go,
  Seeing nothing on their way.

Skies to them are ever blue ;
  Autumn much the same as Spring :
All is old, and nothing new ;
  Birds are birds, and they should sing.

Is it not so ?—yet I feel
  Oft impelled to halt awhile,
Where the silvery brooklets steal
  Out into the sun, and smile.

Whence this subtile sympathy
  'Twixt dull matter and the mind,
And which, moving aye in me,
  Is not common to my kind.

B

Not in any school was taught
The sweet trick of doing so,
Nature woos me, and the thought
Tells it if I write or no.

Nov. 11th, 1875.

———

THE SPIRIT OF THE SPRING.

SWEET Spirit of the Spring,
I hear thee on the wing;
I saw thee leave thy darling where the snowdrops shed
their light;
And I heard thee, singing, say,
Come, love, with me away,
And I'll chant a sweeter matin as we sunward take
our flight.

I will show thee where the lilies,
The laughing daffodillies,
Are bright with golden halos and bending o'er the
brooks,
Whose pretty, playful ways
Have scooped out fairy bays
In the willow-wattled bank-side and by alder-shaded
nooks.

Come say, love, wilt thou follow,
Over height and primrose hollow?
I will give thee in a solo **the heart's** sweet overflow,
Till the merle takes up the **chorus**,
As the zephyrs whisper o'er us,
" O most pleasant 'tis to **warble where the** daffodillies
grow."

Sweet Spirit of the Spring,
'Tis heaven to hear thee sing,
For spring, **with flowers and** sunshine, and the **merry
lark** away,
Were **but an eyeless** Grace,
With the soul out of her face,
Though **our children light the** meadows and frisky
lambkins play.

MY BEAUTIFUL LAND OF THE WEST.

SONG.

The Cingalese boast of their isle,
With its citron and cinnamon-groves,
Where the brightest of summer-suns smile,
And Joy in **a** Paradise roves ;
I know it is fragrant and fair,
Its charms have been ever confessed,
But no spot with my own can compare—
My beautiful land of the West.

Of the far away region of **Ind,**
  The swarthy skinned children **sing ;**
As their bungalows home to their **mind**
  Their memories lovingly bring ;
But vain **are** the groves of **Cashmere,**
  With maidens all gorgeously **dressed,**
They vanish whenever appear
  The dreams **of my** beautiful West.

They say that the thrushes are mute,
  If Philomel thither **doth stray,**
And pensively trills, **like a lute,**
  The notes of her pastoral lay ;
No marvel ! so strange is her song,
  Regretful to leave, and distressed,
Her burden the day and night **long**
  Is, " Beautiful land of **the West."**

FLORAL FELLOWSHIP.

O, FLOWERS ! so mutely eloquent,
Whose lips ambrosial breathe the scent
Of Eden in Earth's primal days—
When Eve to Adam sang your praise

In virginal and sweetest song,
With unpolluted heart and tongue.—
Ye have two worshippers to-day !
The ardent sun, whose golden ray
Your halo makes, an aureole
Of glory, giving to the whole
A beauty so immaculate,
I hold you all inviolate.
Speak, fair one ! from the sunny Loire,
Close neighbouring by Dijon's "Gloire ;"
And thou, the "Duke," with radiant crest,
And "Prince Camille" in crimson drest ;
Thou, too, celestially serene,
Of white rosebuds the Bride and Queen ;
And lastly, thou the crowning one,
Whose soul-born passion for the sun
Hath made thee, blushing to the core,
Of rapt delight the cynosure !
Thou passing fair and odorous thing,
Love's blossom with betrothal ring,
In mossy mantelet arrayed,
And dearer than the "Bourbon" maid ;
What is your ministry below ?
It must be one of grace, I trow.
But as I write your petals fall,
To deck your own sweet funeral—
Which makes me half unconscious sigh
To think such lovely things must die.

Thus full of gratitude, that we
Have shared your love and purity ;
And that, when you have ceased to **live,**
You still will sweetest odour give,
I, lacking the magician's **art**
To stay the fell destroyer's **dart,**
Would fain embalm you in a line,
And so your subtile charms enshrine.

THE SPRING O' THE DAWN.

SONG.

O ! HAVE you been up when the spring **o'** the dawn
With its glow lights the green on the brow o' the lawn,
Ere the "bell" o' the buck wakes the doe, with her
    fawn
    To hear the lark's song in the morning ⸮

The bonny wee warbler, refresh'd with his **rest,**
"Good morrow !" lilts out to his love in her nest,
While pluming his pinions and rearing his crest
    To welcome the light o' **the** morning.

Now fluttering his wings, all bedabbl'd with dew,
He soars up the grey for a sight o' the blue,
Loud singing **his** song, until lost **to** the view,
    His first merry song in **the** morning.

So it's O ! to be out in the spring o' the dawn,
When the glare o' the grey greens the grass on the
    lawn,
Ere the bellowing buck wakes the doe, with her fawn,
    To hear the gay lark in the morning.

MAIDENHOOD.

TO ROSE.

MAIDENHOOD'S the May of life,
    Charming, bright, and sweet sixteen ;
Little care and little strife,
    Hope, and heart, and fancy green.

Then the rose is partly blown,
    Love's most captivating lure ;
Life a dulcet semitone,
    And the lily-bell is pure.

Soft enchantments everywhere,
    Work their spells upon the soul ;
Earth bewitches—Heaven is fair,
    All is bliss from pole to pole.

Take thy pleasure, Rose, to-day,
    Harvest sunshine for thy gloom ;
Know December makes no hay,
    Meadows do not ever bloom.

DOROTHY.

A NEW YEAR'S HANDSEL.

A LITTLE living flash of light !
She met my gaze a year ago ;
Lithe, golden-lock'd, in blue and white,
With forehead like the virgin snow,
Joy gave his jewels for her eyes ;
And such a grace was in her mien,
I stood entranc'd with rapt surprise !
And idoliz'd the tiny queen.
Methinks I hear her bird-like call,
When I enshrin'd her as my saint ;
And see the legends in the hall,
That decorate her palace quaint.
In olden English "East or West,"
For them Contentment did bestead,
Was o'er the hearth with " Hame is best,"
And " Give us Lord our daily bread."
It was a literary " meet "
A sweet exchange of courtesies ;
And as we took our homeward beat,
Along a lane with pleasant trees,
A friend this simple question ask'd,
" You saw that pretty thing at play,
Wilt have her little life unmask'd " ?

Then sauntering upon the way
"A strange romance indeed," he said,
"As strange as aught thine ears can hear,
  Is thrown around that little maid,"
  The tale—whose finis is a tear.

" The merry mass was nearly o'er,
  The moon was frozen in the sky ;
  Deep lay the snow upon the moor ;
  And stars were shiv'ring in the sky :—
  The owl in yonder hollow tree,
  Ne'er ventur'd forth in search of prey ;
  And silence could not deader be,
  That hour before the New Year's day.
  When lo ! a peasant passing by,
  Returning from the ringing feast,
  Heard a long faint and tremulous cry,
  Unlike the wail of bird or beast ;
  And halting for awhile the sound
  Came with the driving sleet again ;
  When nearing it behold he found
  A little babe upon the plain.
  Hard was his hand, but soft his heart,
  He clasp'd the infant to his breast,
  And proud to play a parent's part,
  He made the little thing a nest.
  There ! that's the place, and that's the brick,
  That made its pillow, which you see ;"

Then leaping o'er the fencing, quick
He broke a portion off for me.
I see the very spot in Kent,
Hard by a village church it lies,
With ancient lichgate weather-rent ;
And yew-grove barring out **tho skies.**
But to his **story.** " Love is love
And 'tis the sweetest thing on earth ;
Know nothing could **the** infant move,
Or make it show a sign of mirth ;
And so, **of** course, when daylight came,
The ' find ' was rumour'd far and near ;
And many **a** maid, and married dame,
Call'd in, and dropp'd soft pity's tear :
Still **not a** token gave **the** child
That it was pleas'd, **or** satisfied,—
Until yon **lady on** it smil'd,
When lo ! **to lift its** hands it tried.
She bending lower down, it clung
Around her fair and **slen**der neck ;
When the sweet lullaby was sung,
As **tears ran** down, **a** tiny beck.
' Heaven's will be done,' the lady said,
' I have **no** child, **I'll** cherish thee.'
The foundling is that blue-eye'd maid,
God's gift—they **nam'd her** Dorothy."

THE PINNACLE OF FAME.

Would'st mount it? know 'tis next the sky!
  And when 'tis reach'd, 'tis hard to stand
Observ'd by every curious eye
  That seeks a wonder in the land.

The glowworms light their little fires,
  Unharm'd in the untrodden ways;
While lighthouse-lamps and temple-spires
  Attract the levin's deadly blaze.

So hear, before thou dost ascend,
  If thou must climb its slipp'ry steep;
Small danger little souls attend,
  The fall of great men is sea-deep.

WOMAN'S STRENGTH.

Who ever had a thought of might
  When speaking of the flowers?
We only think of the delight
  They give in sunny hours;
Or how, when heaven is black with gloom,
  And human hearts are sad,
We bear them to the sick one's room
  To make the spirit glad.

Yet lilies bending to the blast,
   Are delicately strong ;
And fledglings as the storms sweep past
   Will suffer little wrong.
The lark sits closer to her **nest**
   As beats the pelting rain ;
For there's **a** fire within her breast,
   That never glows **in vain.**

The force of feeble helplessness,
   What hero can withstand ?
The little infant's fond caress
   Makes strong the heart and hand.
And O ! what power is in a smile,
   And might in simple words !
E'en whispers can our woes beguile
   And charm like happy birds.

What so defenceless as a dove,
   Or little meek-eyed lamb ?
And yet we keep the first for love,
   And when, without its **dam,**
The orphan wean bleats on the waste,
   How potent is its voice
To make the faithful shepherd haste,
   And bid its heart rejoice.

So, weakness is a woman's strength,
  She, powerless to defend
Herself, will own the man at length
  Her best and bravest friend ;
Yet when in times of sore distress,
  His hope despairing flies—
Strong in her love and tenderness
  She saves him or she dies.

THE LITTLE BLIND LAMB.

HE who hath open eyes may see
  God's care is over all ;
This lovely truth was taught to me
  One April festival—

When earth was green, and heaven was blue,
  And with prismatic light,
There shone in every drop of dew
  A little jewel bright.

"Come, let us o'er the stile, across
  The meadow to the dell,
Where Oberon's shield, with golden boss
  Blows by the moschatel."

Thus spake my friend ; I followed, when
  He whispered as he led,—
" You see those sheep on yonder plain,"
  " I do," I softly said.

" Well, when we near that little lamb,
  That's feeding there apart
Without the care of gentle dam,
  Be cautious lest it start."

I watched the little lonely thing,
  Wee orphan of the flock ;
Until it reached a tiny spring
  That bubbled from a rock.

And then it gave a plaintive bleat,
  To which no answer came,
And oft and oft did it repeat
  The cry, the very same.

When lo ! a sound as of a bird,
  At which it pricked its ears ;
And then a kindly voice I heard
  Dispelling all its fears.

" What ails my pretty ? Hither pet ; "
  It wriggled first its tail,
A sight I never shall forget,
  Then sniffed the odorous gale.

And springing with a thrill of love,
  Sped swiftly o'er the ground ;
And answering its friend above,
  Kept straight towards the sound.

"Just go you on, with noiseless tread,"
  Said he, "and bear in mind,
Don't get, if you would pat its head,
  Between it and the wind."

In following my friends behest,
  I marked the pretty thing
Of the sweet herbage, cropped the best
  That clothed the fields of spring.

But as the space that did divide
  Us less and lesser grew,
A sight pathetic, I espied,
  As ever met my view.

The little, sightless, innocent,
  Sore startled by its fear,
Appeared to see my whole intent,
  And eye me with its ear :

For back, towards a purling rill,
  As I advanced, it stept,
And, keeping the same distance still,
  Itself in safety kept.

Another signal, from my friend,
    At which it made a bound ;
And hastened to the further end,
    Delighted at the sound.

And having pressed him with its head,
    Obedient to command ;
"**There's not** a thing but loves," he **said**,
    "**To feel** the human **hand**."

Then did **I** learn, **for** evermore,
    From that poor lambkin's state,—
That Heav'n hath aye a joy **in store**,
    To cheer a hapless fate.

THE DIVINE HARMONY OF THINGS.

HE who made all things well, hath all ordained ;
    Harmonious change is His most stedfast plan :
Great sinners' love is ever most unfeigned ;
    And God's bright glory **most is** seen in man ;
His mercy shone, when he was under ban :
    Hills rise out of the valleys, yet we see
    Without the valleys no huge hills there be.

When lands lie fallow, Nature's force is rife ;
  Upon her couch, the earth is taking rest,
The Winter sleeps, that spring-time, fresh with life,
  May **rear her** flowers, and be with joyance blest.
The bird, of shrivelled leaves, makes cosiest **nest**.
  Without the setting comes no rising sun ;
  And night shows not her stars till day is **done !**

The bitter draught, more welcome makes the **sweet ;**
  Forgiveness hath no **virtue,** without wrong ;
The slow wayfarer tireth out **the** fleet ;
  And he **thinks** deepest, **with a** silent tongue ;
The bird **that sings is captured for its** song ;
  While **those that mute be, know no** captive's pain ;
  And **humblest souls, the highest** heavens **gain.**

Harborne, **December,** 14th. 1870.

THE LILY.

TO TOTTIE.

See'st thou the pretty fairy curl
  Of this sweet lily, named the " Queen " ?
Each odorous petal is **a** pearl
  Set round a heart of gold and green.
So **be thou** too, a vestal white,
  And incense bearer of the light.

c

THE THREE GRACES.

Deborah Dove, and Josephine,
Tripping o'er the village green,
Oh ! how beautiful the pair !
And the maids are debonair.
Deborah's a proud brunette,
Josephine a blonde coquette;
Fairy twins ! now tell to me
Which my favourite will be?

Fairer than the summer-sheen,
Is the lovely Josephine ;
.With **a** blue, bewitching **eye,**
Changing ever, like the **sky.**
Deborah's **lustre is the light**
Of the levin in the night ;
Flashing **with as fine** a scorn
As an eagle's **in the** morn.

Josephine has slender hands,
Delicate as lily-wands ;
Lips, as the carnation sweet ;
And the daintiest of feet.
Deborah is firmly knit,
Strong of hand, and keen of wit ;
And, unmoved as Mona's rock,
Braves the fiercest tempest-shock.

Deborah Dove, and Josephine,
Two such maids are rarely seen ;—
Deborah, the **dark** brunette,
Josephine, the blonde **coquette** ;
But the rose of innocence,
Dora ! with her love intense,
Who entranced me yester-e'en,
Deborah shames, and **Josephine.**

July 31st, 1870.

———

WORSHIP.

SAY, what is worship, but a sense
  Of holy joy, that love is born ;
That **interfusing** effluence
  Of heav'n which glorifies the morn.
Some lovely vision **takes** the sight,
  Some **vestal in her virgin charms,**
Chaste Dian with her silver light,
  Or babe inviolate in arms,
Or Love's fair lady-rose, Celine,
  In lily lustre, may be seen ;
When Rapture, radiant, flaps her wings,
And all around with music rings.

A WAYSIDE CALL.

" It is not good to be alone,"
  Thus said the High and Holy One,
    Of our first father's state ;
And so I felt to-day, as I
In solitude went musing by
    Thy old familiar gate.

And hence I've dropped in just to see,
If thou wilt bear me company,
    For one short hour or so ;
I know thy philosophic mind,
And that to list, thou art inclined ;
    But let us up and go.

As one by one the flowers appear,
To calender the rolling year,
    'Tis well and wise to mark,
That beauty is the aim and end
Of all that nature does, my friend ;
    Nor gropes she in the dark :—

Progressively, by devious ways,
She here a tint or form displays,
    Her purpose to disclose ;
Perfection running up the range,
By an eternal law of change,
    To the consummate rose.

Behold it, in its blushing pride
And glory, as the summer's bride,
    And idol of the sun !
And catch the incense of its breath,
Then sigh with me, that ruthless death
    Will claim so fair a one.

And yet perchance, it may be so,
That flowers that come, and fading go,
    More perfect are above ;
As death, that took that babe of thine,
No longer mortal, but divine,
    Diviner made thy love.

MY REPLY.*

WHAT do I think of Devon now?
   I would, my friend, that I could tell,
For joy beats wild within my brow,
   And speech is holden with a spell.

From Twyford-town† to Tamer-tide,
   And Berry Head to Barum Pool,
I love its dear old country side,
   In rustic phrase, both "mor and mool." ‡

And every lyn, hoe, **tor,** and strand,
   Bluff, **river,** wood, and rocky lane,
Cliff, **close,** croft, carn, and beach o' sand,
   'Tween Babbicombe and Barricane.

I am a child among the flowers,
   My love did ever lean that way,
With them I deck my singing bowers,
   And with them all my fancies **play.**

And so, **for** very shame, I blush,
   To think I e'er forsook her **charms** ;
Sweet Paradise of lark and thrush,
   Where Beauty waits with open arms ;

---

* Written on my return from Ilfracombe, North Devon.
† Ancient name of Tiverton.
‡ Root and Mould.

And hedgerows, built **of fuschias, stand,**
  With crimson droplets hanging down
In graceful trails **along** the land,
  O'er sedgy banks with mosses brown.

My **checks are** burning as I write,
  That, living in so bleak a spot,
I thought **not that her** myrtle bright
  Bloomed ever in its garden knot.

That the verbena, here **a dwarf,**
  Grew there into a towering **tree,**
And hung aloft its fragrant **scarf,**
  O'er lavender and rosemary.

And the arbutis, rich in bloom
  And crimson berries, are her boast ;
And death had not the **power to doom**
  The rose to wither **on her coast.**

But how **can I depict in song**
  The escallonia **in its** pride ?
Whose buds **blush all the winter** long,
  With red **geraniums by its** side :

Or uplands, rich with smiling vines ?
  Or vales, where cream and honey flow ?
And junkets, sweet as native wines ?
  Or **meadows where** the hawthorns blow ?

Then when I sought her balmy shades,
　With primrose tuft, and flashing burn,
And cottages in blue-bell glades,
　With hart's tongue flanked, and lady fern;

Or clambered up the lichened rocks—
　Gold, emerald, orange, grey, and brown;
And scared the rabbit and the fox,
　And hare upon **the** furzy down;

And plucked the wild thyme on her banks,
　And samphire clinging to the crag,
My very being thrilled with thanks,
　And my heart bounded like her stag.

But oh! the music **of** her sea!
　And oh! the **beauty** of her skies!
And what was **dearer far to** me,
　The sparkle **of her** merry eyes!

And cheery words **of** welcome heard,
　In racy tones **from** rich and poor,
Which made my soul sing like a bird,
　And leave a blessing at each door.

Such sweet delights shall make my feast,
　Till I again behold her sun
Arise all glorious in the East,
　And his career unclouded run.

Harborne, October 24th, 1878.

PRO MEMORIA.

BARUM'S BENEFACTOR,

WILLIAM FREDERICK ROCK, **ESQ.**

The music of a merry lay
  Comes warbling from the pleasant West,
  Which wakes an echo in the breast,
And tells of dear ones far away
  Rejoicing, in their love, to greet
The pride and glory of their flock,—
A hero of the purest stock,
  With bounding hearts and dancing feet.

We talk of Paradise above—
  Why not of Paradise below?
  There's joy to reap, but we must sow,—
Exchange the vulture for the dove;
  Seek peace, the antidote of strife;
If we that rich delight would know,
The happiness of those who show
  The sweet humanities of life.

See him whose venerable head
  Irradiates your park to-day !
  Whose thoughts, like little ones at play
Among the hillocks of the dead,
  Are drinking in the golden light
Of beauty, haloing the flowers,
And storing up for after hours
  Bright memories to glad the night.

The sire to his belovèd town
  Another jewel gives to keep,
  A pleasaunce, which shall bless her sleep
With visions, when the sun is down ;
  And round him as fond mothers stand,
They press their babes unto their breast,
And pray that they may be as blest
  As she who gave him to the land.

True poet, citizen, and friend !
  Great, noble, bountiful, and free !
  A type in all the days to be
Of love that loveth to the end.
  Let the fair marble speak his fame,
And verse in monumental song,
For Nature does herself a wrong,
  When silent on a good man's name.

August 12th, 1879.

NOONTIDE.

The air is like a freighted bee,
All redolent of sweets;
And languid, low, and wearily,
The pulse of Nature beats.

A drowsy hum pervades the ground,
With fragrant buds besprent;
And calm-eyed cattle lie around,
The pictures of content.

The breath of life is in the breeze,
Fresh wafted from the South;
While lilac, and laburnum trees,
And hawthorns scent the drouth.

Harborne, 1877.

THE MITHER'S HEART IS WI' 'EM.

Tread softly, for 'tis holy ground;—
A casket is that grassy mound,
Where three wee-jewels o' the heart,
Are laid awhile to rest apart
From her who held them more than dear;
So softly tread, in drawing near,
The Mither's heart is wi' 'em.

The winds of heaven were tempered **so,**
That only gentlest airs did blow
Upon their fair love-tended forms,
So sheltered were they from the storms ;
And now since underneath the sky,
Her pretty babes* are doomed to lie,
 The Mither's heart is wi' 'em.

Not always here the bairnies rest,
But **often on** her yearning breast ;
For in the dreams, that night doth bring,
On love's soft, downy-pinion'd wing,
Her spirit from her Northern home,
To fondle them will hither come:—
 The Mither's heart is wi' 'em.

Tread softly then 'tis holy ground !
For tears have hallowed all around :
Here reigns a deep perpetual hush
Unbroken by the lark or thrush,
Since death has consecrated all ;—
Tread softly as the shadows fall,
 The Mither's heart is wi' 'em.

Harborne Churchyard, Feb. 27th, 1877.

---

* The following simple but very touching inscription may be seen on
the little headstone :—

 R. C. R. **1870.**
 M. J. R. 1871.
 J. L. R. 1872.

TO A FORGET-ME-NOT.

FORGET thee, sweetling? list, I pray,
Who that has seen thy face,
My pretty sapphire of the May,
As radiant as a summer-ray ;
But must remember thee for aye,
While memory holds her place.

Forget thee? look up at the night,
And watch the love-star glow ;
The moon too robed in silver-white,
Can'st thou forget that they are bright?
Then hear me, O, my soul's delight,
Can I forget thee? No !

Forget thee? dost thou e'er forget
That summer hath her flowers?
They trust the sun and ne'er regret
And if, like thine, their eyes grow wet,
They only pay love's common debt,
And sweeter make the hours.

Forget thee? jewel of my heart !
If I were e'en thy foe,
I'd rush against the fatal dart
Hurled at thy breast with deadly art ;
Alas ! my love, that we must part.
Can I forget thee? No !

SANCTIFIED SORROW.

As just before the break of day,
   Impatient of the night,
The skylark, on his heavenward **way,**
   Sings sweetest in his flight,
So minstrels chant their purest strains,
   When from affliction's room
Faith soars to her celestial plains,
   Afar from sorrow's gloom.

Then murmur not if thou art told,
   When pain shall lay thee low,
That stricken souls yield finest gold,
   In crucibles of woe.
And Sorrow's sister, Sympathy,
   With balsam for each wound,
Would ne'er on earth an angel be,
   Without some thorny ground.

No picture's possible to sense
   That is devoid of shade;
'Tis blank and barren all, and hence
   Fair beauty is unmade;
But let the painter's magic wand,
   Be waved athwart the **white,**
Then shadow, balanced by his hand,
   Reveals the soul of light.

The planets touch not, as they roll
  Their holy altar fires,
The finer issues of the soul,
  Until the moon retires ;
And oft the peerless Queen of stars,
  Most glorious doth shine,
When a dark cloud her passage bars,
  Which makes her all divine.

The Spring is very beautiful,
  Which brings the Summer day ;
And bounteous, fair and dutiful,
  The Autumn wends her way :
But not a lillybell had blest
  The Summer's sunny eyes,
Or Autumn worn her golden crest,
  But for the frozen skies.

Then trust in God, and come what will,
  Sun, shadow, storm or shine,
He reigneth, on His heavenly hill,
  All-loving and benign :
Know Mercy's other name is Change ;
  And when our work is done,
She comes, as Death, and bids us range
  The region of the sun.

May 22nd, 1878.

I SAID TO MY LOVE.

SONG.

I SAID to my love " I will tarry for thee,"
As he told me his fortune **lay** over the sea,
When thus, he replied, as he gazed in mine eyes,
Spellbound in **a** sweet and **ecstatic surprise** :

" Thy faith is as fair as thy lily-white hand ;
  But vows are **like** characters **writ on** the sand :—
  The isle where the Cingalese **dwell is** afar,
  And the ocean, dear maid, is a measureless bar."

" The vow on the sand-beach will vanish 'tis true,
  But the heart that is loyal ne'er heeds an ' adieu.'
  The ocean I know is a waste deep and wide,
  But nothing can love-wedded spirits divide."

" My ship may set sail with a prosperous wind,
  But leave thee, my jewel, in sorrow behind ;
  For the wrenching asunder of natures like **ours**
  Is death to the heart, as the blast to the flowers."

" **Thy** ship may set sail with a prosperous breeze,
  And bear my delight far away **o'er** the seas ;
  But the hope **of** true love has **a** life in its spark,
  Which faith keepeth ever alit in the dark."

" The rack may come **racing**, and cruel winds blow,
And send thy love whither no **mortal doth know** ;
And **never a word** or a token be **found**
To tell of the fate of his **bark**, or the **drowned**."

" The rack **may** come on with its death-dealing frown,
And the hurricane storm, **and the vessel go down** ;
But love ne'er believes **where** the eye cannot see,
And living **or** dead I will tarry for thee."

October 13th, **1877.**

THE MERRY BARKERS.

LIST ! 'tis the sturdy woodman, hark !
As merry as a mounting lark ;
How **musical he** makes the air
While eyeing the old giant there !

" Hurrah ! **hurrah ! my** comrades all !
Our Forest-king to day must fall.
His crest no **more** shall sweep the sky,
The grand old **oak is** doomed to die.

" **Oft** has his gaunt and noble form,
Stood buffeting the wind and storm ;
When bonny greenwoods found a den,
For **hungry** wolves and hunted men.

D

" Though gnarled and knotted to the core,
And friend of many a savage boar,
All proudly he his head has borne,
He falls—to rise no more this morn."

With trusty twibill now they go,
Groping about his roots below ;
Which chopped, they deftly ring the bole,
And then commence to fell him whole.

Whilst high aloft the bright axe swings,
From hill to hill the echo rings ;
Till quivering with the fatal blow,
The ruthless wedges lay him low.

Down with a shock and wild rebound,
He **sends** the thundering signal round ;
And **'ere his last** death-throes are o'er,
His brawny limbs bestrew the floor.

Close following **their** fallen prey,
The loppers' tools begin to play ;
Nor cease till with **a** heavy thud
Prone lies the last **bough,** quick with bud.

Now glistening in the May-day sun,
The ripping irons nimbly run ;
Until the veteran huge and fair,
Lies with his twisted muscles bare.

Meanwhile the fragrant rind is seen,
Thick standing on the flowery green,
To catch the sun and **drying wind,**
While chips the thrifty setters find.

As thus their busy hands they ply,
The **sultry** day begins to die,
When **the** old oak is left at rest,
To bleach upon his mother's breast.

And now, as home they wend their way,
Some ancient sings a simple lay ;
Then wets his whistle **with** a horn,
And prays for a good-morrow morn.

TO " PRUDENTIA."

As yestere'en, **behind his icy bars**
The glinting sun **flush'd all** around with light,
A dazzling speck **of ruby met my** sight
More radiant than **the roseal hue** of Mars.
And while it, fading, **died before** the night,
I **watch'd** it, listening to the even-chime,
And thought upon that memorable time
When Bethlehem's glory lit the orient skies.

Just then a vision pass'd before mine eyes,
More fair than in those late December days
When Earth was one enchanting Paradise
Of woodlands sparkling with white coral sprays.
I saw thee leave thy place among the stars,
And swift descending, as the meteor darts,
Alight an angel **in** our western ways ;
A presence stilling all discordant **jars,**
And pouring balsam into **wounded hearts.**
Much more saw I, of which I took good heed ;
Though thou wert often **like the** bruiséd reed.
I saw thee with pale Sorrow's taper light,
In the still watches of a winter night—
Soft gliding to the sick **couch** smilingly,
And making it the crown of thy delight
In soothing suffering to tranquillity.
Too well I know thou need'st not this from **me,**
Since joy is born of every kindly deed,
And that to thee is more than royal meed :
This much confess I too most willingly,
Words are but empty bearers of my thought,
And love needs none for that which love hath wrought;
Still were I mute the very stones would **cry**
Behold the ingrate ! **to each passer by.**
I know, sweet lady, blessing much and blest,
No pen can **all** the heart's true feeling tell ;
Its office is a failure, at the best,
But thou on the intent wilt fondly dwel'.—

And as the queenly moon, with royal grace,
When the bright sun has vanish'd with his light,
Reflects his chaster beauty on her face
And shows it to our wondering eyes at night,—
So wilt thou, too, a fairer charm bestow
Upon my song, and make my joy o'erflow,
When on thy bosom thou shalt wear my lay,
As love's pearl-lily, for thy natal day.

Christmas, Eve, 1878.

———

THE SPIRIT OF BEAUTY.

O ! sweet enchantress of the heart
I feel thy presence everywhere !
I meet thee on the windy brake,
I see thee when the stars awake,
Thou art my being's fairer part,
And spirit of earth, sea, and air.
I've revelled in thy realms of bliss,
Rapt worship, wonder and delight,
And gave to thee my virgin kiss,
When thou wert sovereign of the night.
And when the wild gull swept the sky
And gleamed out, like a star, on high,
I lay upon the beach in June,

While Ocean played his dulcet tune,
And sought thee in each silver cloud,
And found thee, a bright angel there ;
Unnoticed, by **the** gadding crowd,
But palpable, and passing fair,
To me, who in each speck could view
Thy **form** celestial in the blue.

WEST AND SOUTH.

So fair the both,
To choose I'm loth,
But truth for aye,—
So list my lay.

O ! I love the bonny **West** !
With her lilies on her breast,
Making **odorous** the dells,
With **the incense of her bells,**
While the **young** grass groweth sweet,
To the tramp of little feet,
   Dancing aye O !
   In May O !

And the soft and sunny South !
With her rosebud in her mouth,
As the perfume of the flower,
She is breathing on the hour
When the sun is making hay,
Where men and maidens play,
    Singing " June-O " !
    In tune, O !

    So sweet the both,
    To choose I'm loth,
    The truth for aye,--
    I love the " tway."

New Year's week, 1880.

HOME TREASURES.

Blessings evermore I say
On those little ones at play.

What a charming group of graces !
See them with their happy faces,
Joy of joys, and bliss of blisses,
I could smother them with kisses.

Joy is there that knows no measure,
Pleasure, yes, divinest pleasure !
Love's own round of dear employment,
Constant toiling, rapt enjoyment ;
Pleasure in sweet variation,
Pleasure in anticipation.
Ere they share our fond caresses
Hope in these our being blesses ;
Dimpled chins, and cheeks, and eyes,
Bluer than the bluest skies ;
Little fat hands, plumpy feet,
Little lips with pouting sweet ;
Tiny tongues, so strangely talking,
Tiny feet unused to walking ;
Fingers playing with each other,
Sweet epitomes of mother !
Tell me not of the majestic,
Give to me the dear domestic—
Little boys with glossy tresses,
Little maids in milk-white dresses.
O ! the music of the rattle,
With its bells and baby prattle ;
Babblement of little Babel,
Music of the wicker cradle !
Children !—did you ever see
Such a pure democracy ?
Mark the little dears at play
On some sunny summer day,

Burying their hands in daisies,
Carolling the sweetest praises ;
Some with ringlets, bright and jetty,
Others auburn—sweetly pretty :
Some with ruddy apple cheeks,
And an eye that almost speaks ;
Some **with** radiant golden curls,
Laughing boys, and romping girls ;
But of all the sights one sees
In creation, give me these :
First a mother, more than **blest,**
With her baby at her **breast ;**
Next infantile piety
Lisping at a mother's knee ;
Last of all, the sweetest, **best,**
Putting the sweet things to rest.
See the little cuddling creatures
With their love-illumined features.
There is Dora, aged seven,
Like a cherub fresh from heaven ;
" Kiss me, mother," **chirrups Lucy ;**
And, with **lips like cherries** juicy,
Little Nelly **asks the same ;**
Lilian, prettier than her name,
Shakes her curls upon her pillow,
Wild as sun-rays on a billow ;
Milly sings herself to sleep,
Charlie wants his dogs and sheep ;

Jess is happy with her dolly ;
And wee Fred's the doll for Polly.
Now the mother tucks them in,
" Where," quoth she, " shall I begin ? "
" Me, me, me, dear mother, me,"
Shout aloud the elder three.
But, despite their earnest prayer,
First the youngest claims her care.
Hear her sing her lullaby,
Mark her in her fondness sigh,
List her " By-bye, precious treasures,
God I thank Thee for these pleasures ;
Bless their slumbers, calm their **fears.**
Good night, **pretties,** good night, **dears.**"
" Good night, mother," all reply ;
" Now all go to seepy by."
And then comes the crowning bliss,
Mother's smile and parting kiss.
Oh, an angel is a mother!
Little children ask no other.

A SIGH FOR DEVON.

BRIGHT haunt of the daffodil, myrtle, and **rose**,
Of solitude sweet, and of pleasant repose,
Where **a welcome** waits all with a heart in its **hand**,
My Devon ! **dear Devon ! my** beautiful land !
May death **ne'er for thee draw** a shaft **from his**
    quiver,
I loved thee, **do love, and shall love** thee for ever.

Dear home **of my fathers, when thinking of thee,**
In fancy **I often am** down by **the sea,**
On old **Northam** Burrows, or Woolacombe sands,
Where Robert **the** phantom is twisting **his bands.**
Then deem **me** no runnaway-ingrate, O never !
First love of my **heart, I shall** love thee for ever.

When summer is come, and the welkin is fair,
There's something of paradise everywhere ;
But **bloom in** perfection, and nature **in** tune,
Are thine, O Devonia ! in beautiful June.
Blest region **of** valley, hill, woodland, and river,
I love thee, dear land, and shall love thee for ever.

The meadows o' Warwick are dainty and sweet,
And the fair fields o' Staffordshire, soft to the feet;
But for rich mossy sward, sunny upland, and glen,
Lane, coppice, and stream, give me Devon **again**.
Yes! soul-bound to thee, which no fate can dissever,
I love thee, dear land, and shall love thee for **ever**.

Thanks Memory, nurse o' my fancy and hope,
I **feel** I am now where the combes are aslope,
While innocent lovers are **telling** their tale,
At Barricane beach and in Collipriest vale,
Where **my Exe** from **the** moorland weds Lowman's
    fair river :—
Sweet land of my love ! I shall love thee for **ever**.

PHEMIE, THE FAIR.

O ! KNOW you the ditty of Phemie the **Fair**,
Not Helen o' Harborne, nor Winnie o' Ware,
Nor Lyd o' the Leasowes, **nor Pat o' the** Peak,
To measure their charms, as her rivals dare seek.
For the lassie was lissome, and bonny, and sweet,
With the whitest o' hands and the weeest o' feet ;
And her voice like **the** linnet's, could charm away
    care,
But pride never whispered her, " Phemie is Fair."

And her manner was winsome, and sunny her face,
As she walked on the earth, like an angel o' grace ;
A presence o' gladness, a light, and a joy,
And fate suffered nothing her life to annoy.
A flower o' true modesty, made to allure
The gentle in nature, the noble, and pure ;—
The rudest and roughest to gaze would forbear,
As they passed in the meadows, sweet " Phemie the
    Fair."

In the hush of the hour, when the sun on the wane
Gives a rich golden glow to the wood and the lane,
She walked, a live lily, in raiment o' white,
The image of beauty, and perfect delight.
And oft she would gaze with a far-away look,
And read the bright heavens as they were a book,
Till her soft moulded lips showed the motion of
    prayer,
For so she would worship, sweet " Phemie the Fair."

'Twas summer ! bright summer ! and down in the vale,
The newly made windrows were scenting the gale ;
As the young and the old full o' spirit and play,
Made light o' their toil, as they tedded the hay ;
When over the pleasant green meadow-land by,
A form like an angel, they chanced to espy,
But as it tript onward, lo ! one unaware
Looked up, and half sighing breathed " Phemie *is*
    Fair."

'Twas summer ! bright summer ! **alas** ! it was so,
Give ear for dear pity, and let the **tear flow** ;
For a storm in the welkin was gathering then,
And the maiden will never see summer again.
The bolt swift descending, **too** fatal it flew,
The shaft of **the** levin shot **red** through the blue ;
When quicker than lightning young Ronald **was**
    there,
With a noble heart broken, for " Phemie the **Fair.**"

" **O !** sorrow **of** sorrows !" **was heard** on the wind,
" **O !** sorrow **of** sorrows ! the maiden is blind !"
O ! **grief and O** sorrow ! **she** speaks, and he cries,
" Alas ! **for my** darling !" and staggers, and dies.
And ever in June, there the maiden is **seen,**
With her fair locks dishevell'd, slow pacing the green,
Distraught and low singing, " Where's Ronald ? O
    where ? "
While neighbours **sigh** wistly " **Poor Phemie the**
    Fair."

Harborne, October 14th, **1877.**

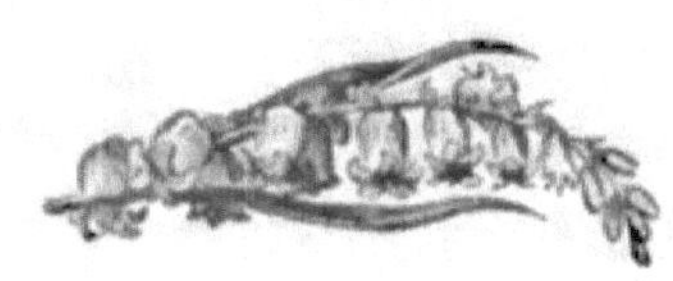

TO JANIE,

WITH A LILY OF THE VALLEY.

ACCEPT this firstling of her race,
  This devotee of vernal flowers.
See, worship beameth in her face,
  And praise is heard in all her bowers,
Sweet silent syllables of song,
The odours of her perfumed tongue.

But list, my dear, the little saint
  Doth almost ask a cloistered cell,
Where she may live, secure from taint,
  And ring her little holy bell ;
And so it shames me, for I found
Her blooming where the " blacks " abound.

Thus love, from every object, we
  May learn a wholesome lesson rare,
Sun, star, bird, butterfly, and bee,
  And little floweret frail and fair,
Of courage, and the part to play
As actors in the evil day.

Harborne, June 8th, 1879.

TO A ROSEBUD.

IMPERIAL beauty ! since the muse inclines
To sing thy praise, in sweet thought-laden **lines**,
I take my lyre, and wake its silver strings
To music, floating with soft rosy wings.

Thou fair enchantress ! born of summer skies,
Entrancing all, the simple and the wise ;
Bright child ! whose odour is a seraph's breath ;
Earth's richest relic, from **the** wreck of death.

Quintessence of all loveliness ! a shrine
Where reverent spirits worship the divine ;
As in the pauses of each happy bird,
The still small voice of prophecy is heard.

The charms of all the **ages meet in thee** ;
The roseate blushes of their morns **we see** ;
And the rich tintings of their gorgeous eves
Are subtly mingled in thy folded leaves.

O peerless blossom ! how the raptured sight
Views heaven's own landscape with poetic light !
As fancy treads thy labyrinthine streets,
And sips the nectar of thy hidden sweets.

Who has not seen in summer's sunny days,
Thy heart thrown open to the golden rays ?
Where nestling close they set thy soul aflame,
And crimsoned o'er thy cheek with love's pure shame.

And O, the sounds that greet our list'ning ear,
As by thy fragrant lips we linger near ;
The soft sweet whisperings of dreamy trees,
And the low hum of honey-laden bees.

And then what fairy visions meet our eyes !
Of sylph-like forms, ethereal butterflies ;
And golden beetles seeking thee, to rest
In the sweet chamber of thy perfumed breast.

Love claims a song to sing them, but in vain,
For half thy charms, unsung, must still remain ;
Yet this the muse can do, in secret sigh,
That thou, who art so beautiful, must die.

BEAUTY.

An affluent of the stream of life,
  As opal, fair and crystalline,
To bless the barren waste of strife,
  And make the wilderness divine.

F

OLD CALEB TO HIS FRIENDS.

Let mirth come with the mistletoe
  Though sorrow follow after,
Since He who feeds the fount of tears
  Fills every heart with laughter;
Know if holly-thorns mean trials sore,
  The berries speak of joys,
And they always grow together,
  My merry maids and boys.

TO THE SUN.

Great eye of nature! at whose glance
The songsters of the morning dance!
Supremest light, which doth afar
Gild the bright twinklings of the star!
Divinest pencil, from whose touch
The tinted rainbow borrows much!
Thou, who illumest with thy light
The chamber of the Queen of night,
And art of life, light, heat, the soul,
From southern to the northern pole,—
Blind is the man that cannot see
The glory of his God in thee.

Lover's Walk, **Barum**, June, **1845.**

NATURE'S TINTERN ABBEY.

WRITTEN IN HARBORNE CHURCHYARD.

Sweet place of tears ! whene'er I visit thee,
A vision of the bygone haunteth me ;
Which fond remembrance keeps in colours bright,
Embalmed in beauty, as a dear delight :

It is a scene upon the pleasant **Wye,**
Where ivy-mantled ruins meet the eye :
So delicately **airy,** I have thought
To heavenly music all its parts were wrought.

Where Chepstow's donjon overhangs the tide,
I halted once upon a summer ride ;
And having paid it homage, sped away
To hold with Nature her high holiday.

When broke the Wynd Cliff on my ravished sight,
And tripping down from its romantic height,
The queen of crumbling temples met my view,
Fair, pensive, lone, and venerable of hue.

Where anglers oft, forgetful of their prey,
Will turn to watch the light and shadows play ;
Around some monumental column's head,
Or foliated wreck among the dead.

And tired wayfarers halting for awhile,
Will raptured gaze upon the sacred pile ;
And feel compelled, 'ere they pursue their way,
To bend the knee in reverence, and pray.

But nature has her abbeys everywhere ;
And minsters with their aisles divinely fair ;
Grand nave and transept, spire and cloister dim,
And galleries where joyous minstrels hymn.

And since my fate, the pleasure has denied,
To dwell and worship by yon river's side,
Fair grove of Harborne ! I will turn to thee,
And Tintern's Abbey thou shalt be to me ;

For no cathedral reared in olden time,
Can gloom more solemn at the midnight chime,
Than our hypœthral fane upon the hill,
When heaven is mute, and all the earth is still.

Our fathers worshipped underneath the trees ;
And sang their anthems to the passing breeze :
The early morn their pious matin heard ;
And they their vesper chanted with the bird.

Henceforth dear spot, whenever I repair
To nature's temple, bent on praise and prayer,
Or meditation, thou my voice shalt hear,
Since thy most sacred shades I do revere.

1880.

CORA LEE.

SONG.

List the maiden of the mountain,
  Singing her sweet sorrow lay,
To the dripple of a fountain,
  Where the fitful shadows play ;
Singing in a language broken,
  As the storm-waves of the sea,
Notes that saddest thoughts betoken :
  For love-lorn is Cora Lee.

In the flush of life's young morning,
  Tripping o'er the hillocks green,
Every fear and danger scorning,
  She, the pride of all, was seen.
But the love that promised pleasure,
  Only baneful proved to be :
Death stept in and took her treasure,
  And distraught is Cora Lee.

As the hedge-rose of the summer,
  Bright with pink her cheek did glow,
Where the honey-making hummer
  Sought the heather-buds below ;
Now more wan than pallid lily,
  On the wintry morn can be,
Through the long night dark and chilly,
  Woeful plaint makes Cora Lee.

SWEET HETTIE O' CARLOW.

SONG.

SWEET Hettie o' Carlow ! I'm thinking of thee,
Mavourneen, Mavourneen, a cush la machree ;
Thy image is with me, my love and my theme,
And thy melodies haunt me in every dream.
O daughter of Erin ! come hither to me,
Mavourneen, Mavourneen, a cush la machree.

As fair as Killarney, and fresh as the morn,
And blithe as the lark in the spring o' the corn,
I see thee, and hear thee, sweet maiden aga'n ;
And all I can do is to wail the refrain,
" O daughter of Erin ! have pity on me,
Mavourneen, Mavourneen, a cush la machree."

Sweet Jewel o' Carlow ! with soul-killing eye,
This son of my mother heart-broken will die,
If thy foot's pretty patter is heard here no more,
For my soul ran away with thyself through the door.
O daughter of Erin ! come hither to me,
Mavourneen, Mavourneen, a cush la machree.

Harborne, May 4th, 1872.

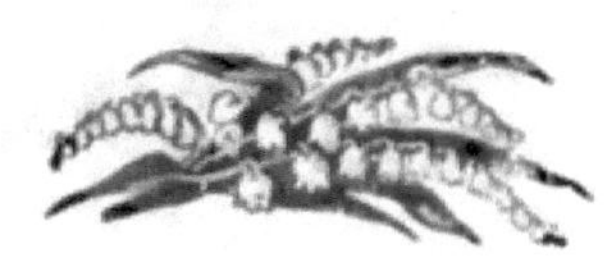

THE MAID O' BONTDDU.*

SONG.

The hills o' Dolgelly with honey are **sweet**,
The bell-heather purples them down to their feet ;
And the sight up the Mawddach is glorious to see,
But I'll sing you a ditty o' fairy Bontddu.

A lad from **the Westland sped** thither one day,
By Chirk and Ruabon, brave, gallant, and gay :
He had heard of **a** maiden, **as** blithe as a bee,
Sweet **Wilhelmy Wynn o' the** pretty Bontddu.

By the deep dykes of Offa **he** shot like a swift,
Or laverock, lilting away **in the lift ;**
The Vale of Llangollen, and sweet water Dee,
And the charms o' Llandrillo, brimful o' Bontddu.

Then the broad lake of Bala he saw in his flight,
But the woods o' Bryntirion† enraptured his sight ;
For there **by the** Mawddach, as fair **as could** be,
Stood Wilhelmy **Wynn**, the delight o' Bontddu.

Her eyes were ripe mazards,‡ and raven her hair,
Each cheek a red **apple, her** forehead snow fair ;
A bonny green kirtle hung down to her knee,
And rapture ran wild **at the Lyn** o' Bontddu.

---

* "**The Black** Bridge," (pronounced " Bontthee.")
† " Pleasant View."
‡ The black cherries of Devon.

Her suitors were many :—Smith, Owen, Rob Moore,
Hughes, Evans, Lloyd, Thomas, and Joneses a score ;
With Roberts, MacDonald, and Andy McCree,
All dying in love for the Rose o' Bontddu.

Still he ventured—"**Dear lass,** I have heard **of your**
      fame ;
A sweet little melody rings in your name."
She chuckled, **and** oh, how bewitching looked **she** !
" Here's another **in** love with the maid o' Bontddu."

Then praising her dimples, he strove for a kiss,
When she cropped his young hope in the bud **of its**
      bliss ;
" Pray stop, pretty bird, you **are** on the wrong **tree** !"
Chirped Wilhelmy Wynn, with the pride o' Bontddu.

He hung down his **head** like a hound in disgrace ;
When with rogue in **each eye, and a blush on her**
      face,
She gave a loud laugh, **but** the ring of **its glee,**
Told a fool was the heart **of the** Maid o' Bontddu.

Love will not be baulked, **so** quoth he, "**Pretty maid,**
Just fancy myself at the **Lyn in your** stead,
And that *you* had come courting far over the lea,
What words would you **woo me with, Maid** o'
      Bontddu ?"

She answered in Welsh, but his patience was gone.
For colder than Snowdon she seemed to look on ;
" I can't understand what you tell me," said he,
" But love has its lure, pretty Maid o' Bontddu."

Then he talked of the Bards, and he piped her a
    stave,
A soul-melting lay of a love-fettered slave ;
When her eyes flashed a light, like the ripples at sea,
That token for rain.   Were there tears at Bontddu ?

Every lane has its turning, and nature will out :
Sweet Wilhelmy chid with the prettiest pout ;
But maids are the same by the Dart and the Deo,
So she pitied the lad that had come to Bontddu.

He saw she was touched, as she coloured and sighed ;
Still love must be wilful, so she, in her pride,
Sang, " Heart, play the hero, and hold thyself free,"
When a keepsake he asked of the Maid o' Bontddu.

Quoth she, " I will give you whenever you leave
A silver-new-nothing to wear on your sleeve."
" A bargain !" he cried, " and I pray you, agree
To seal it at once, pretty Maid o' Bontddu."

Old Cader had put on his cap for the night,
And the cotter's wee window-pane blinked with
    delight,
When a couple went cosy as cosy could be
Up the old road to Harlech, away from Bontddu.

The moon was o'er Dyffryn, and Venus hard by,
Was seen with her silver love-lamp in the sky ;
The stars woo in silence, and silent wooed he,
Life-linked with the beautiful Maid o' Bontddu.

The hills o' Dolgelly with honey are sweet,
The bell-heather purples them down to their **feet ;**
But the girls by the Mawddach are sweeter **to me,**
And **sweetest of all is** the Maid o' Bontddu.

SONG OF THE KEEPER.

Good neighbours draw near,
I've lots of good cheer,
A little of many things pleasant :
I've dainty young roe,
Red deer, buck, and doe,
Hare, partridge, snipe, woodcock, and pheasant.
With my dog and my gun,
I am up 'ere the sun,
Singing songs in the praise of my charmer ;
And leaping the brook,
I scare the black rook,
And rouse up the slumbering farmer.

CHORUS.

Say where is the **dad**
That can boast of a lad
Whose tide of true pleasure runs deeper ;
There is no employ,
For a rollicking boy,
As free as the life of a keeper.

I have Frolic and Rose,
With right tender **nose,**
To spring the brown **bird in September,**
And Missey **and** Bob,
Ever ripe **for** a job,
When we sport in the chilly November.
And Spot, Shot, **and** Rough,
Fan, Billy, and **Bluff,**
To follow me over the furrow.
And sleek as a mole,
There's Vic for a hole,
When the **rabbit is** deep **in his burrow.**

Say where is the dad, &c.

When Winter winds **blow,**
And fair falls the snow,
The pole-cat, the fox, and the badger,
I track with my hound,
Or trap **on the** ground,
And strip off their coats for the cadger.

For catching a stoat,
Or otter afloat,
Owl, **hawk**, kite, and jay, **or** a poacher,
I have always a snare ;
And I'd have those beware,
Who feed the big bags of the troacher.

CHORUS.

So join when I sing,
Like a merry old king,
And drink till your spirits are mellow,
Come, fill up the glass,
Here's health to each **lass,**
And Master, a jolly good fellow.

Buckland Brewer, 1864.

MY VALENTINE.

A LITTLE fair five-hearted thing,
That keeps a pretty golden eye,
To gladden with each coming Spring
The soul of every passer by.

I will not tell my darling's name ;
But if you seek her you will find
She is a very pearl of fame,
And pattern for all womankind.

Her home is in a mossy nook,
    Roofed **over** with young hawthorn bloom,
Out yonder by the waterbrook,
    Where violets the air perfume.

Go ! hear her talk, and see her smile,
    In her own fascinating way ;
And she will win you **with her** wile,
    And make you happier **for aye.**

February 14th, **1880.**

THE "CHARMING" OF THE BIRDS.

SONG.

It is the flowery first o' May !
    Lets **roam among the** heather ;
Enjoying at the **peep o'** day
    The still soft summer weather :
And mark the pale grey border-line,
    Where light and shadow mingle ;
And quaff the air like honey-wine,
    From dairy-cow and dingle.
Hark ! Hey away ! his " Lillelu,"
    The throstle-cock **is sounding** !
Its O ! to brush the bonny dew,
    Where merry stags are bounding.

Who that has felt the witching **power,**
    Life's every care disarming,

When birds in every brake and bower
 Make merry with their " charming,"
And has not strove in tune and time,
 To catch their art of singing ?
And lilted out a note o' rhyme,
 As sweet as love-bell ringing ;
Then, Hey away ! his " Lillelu,"
 The throstle-cock is sounding ;
Its O ! to brush the bonny dew,
 Where merry stags are bounding.

'Tis joy to list the cuckoo's lay,
 From th' umbrageous hollow ;
Before the skylark hails the day,
 And bids the ouzel follow ;
But O ! along the country side,
 Green, daisy-prankt and pearly,
To hear the host at morning-tide,
 Of song birds singing early :
So, Hey away ! his " Lillelu,"
 The throstle-cock is sounding ;
Its O ! to brush the bonny dew,
 Where merry stags are bounding.

YEWLAND.

SONG.

'Tis very strange, how slight a thing
Will touch the heart's most tender string!
Or bid the fancy plume its wing;
And finding it the case to day,
I take my harp, and sing my lay,
The simple song of Yewland.

Don't picture immemorial trees
O'er charnel houses, if you please;
Nor weird owls, hooting to the breeze;
Nor think of bats in haunted halls;
Nor crumbling battlemented walls,
With spectral forms at Yewland.

A home upon a pleasant hill,
Where, in the Spring, the skylarks will
Lead in the dawn with jocund trill;
While thrush and linnet join the song,
Our joy and pleasure to prolong,
Is bonny, bonny Yewland.

A draw-well in a tiny glade;
And seat for the wayfarer made,
Beneath a friendly yewtree's shade;
And wren that builds before the door,
And humming bees in sycamore,
Hath fair and dainty Yewland.

Brown gillies, roses red **and white,**
And southernwood, young love's delight,
And stocks make sweet the summer **night ;**
While, ring'd within its hawthorn fence,
Live Modesty and Innocence,—
The inmates fair of Yewland.

And in a cage, which all might see,
From every care and sorrow free,
A blackbird whistles **merrily**
From early March **to middle June**
The fragment of a ballad-tune,
To please the folk **at Ye**wland.

A sweet epitome **of farms,**
I often **pause** to view its charms,
Of apple-bloom and honey-swarms :
For be it times of rain or drouth,
I find a smile **about the** mouth
Of **those** who dwell at Yewland.

In sooth **I** prize its pretty knot,
And dormer-window'd white-wash'd cot,
Since 'tis an old familiar spot,
Made sacred by the love of yore,
And kindly deeds of one no more,
Who was the life of Yewland.

THE BLUEBELL'S COMPLAINT.

WHAT have I done, O wrathful wind,
　That **thou** so cruel art and cold ?
To thee, **I** have been ever kind,
　And **paid** thy love **a** hundred fold :
I own to feel thy breath was bliss,
But it was perfumed by my **kiss.**

And thou, bright monarch **of** the day !
　Come, **tell me** why thy face is hid,
Why **is** thy ever welcome **ray**
　Obscured by yonder **cloudy lid ?**
No **flower** beneath the **sunny sky**
Can show thy virtue more than I.

Thou, **too,** sweet daughter of the south,
　Whose vesture **is** the tenderest **green,**
Young **Spring with** soft balm-breathing mouth,
　And showers that freshen every scene,
What have **I done to thee, I pray ?**
No bloom have **I,** and yet 'tis **May.**

I long to hear the happy bands
　Of children greet me in **the** lanes ;
And feel their little chubby hands
　Bear **me** in triumph o'er the plains ;
They called me April's gem, but thou
Hast left me lorn and loveless now.

F

THE PRIDE O' THE YEAR.

'Tis buttercup and daisy time
When Summer in her sunny prime,
Beneath her canopy of blue,
Is walking in the early dew ;
And, oh ! what glory to behold
Her sheeny miles of meadow gold.

I love the budding April moon,
And bonny May, but, oh ! when June,
With pearly brow and sapphire eye
And honeysuckle wreath, trips by
In kirtle green and lilac vest,
I feel of all I love her best.

She brings the sweet and swothy days,
When lovers seek the silent ways,
Where birds and golden-belted bees
Sail merrily o'er broomy leas,
And butterflies, in bluebell groves,
In sportive dances woo their loves.

The rosy clover then we view,
The honey-scented bedstraw, too ;
The corn flag in the sunshine waves ;
The wagtail in the runnel laves ;
And jocund blackcap sounds his pipe,
And every hour with joy is ripe.

Then larks essay their highest flight ;
Then Philomela wakes the night ;
Then morns are fresh and eves are cool ;
Then gnats go dancing o'er the pool ;
And dragon-flies, in regal blue,
The winding waterbrooks pursue.

Then woodruff and the meadowsweet
With speedwell and stellarias meet,
And then it is that you may see,
Fair fashioned on the chestnut tree,
The fetlock, hoof, and driven nails,
Nor wonder why the " horse " prevails.

Then days are long and nights are short,
And hedge-hogs find the gipsies sport,
And spottled throstle warbles late
To soothe his little sitting mate ;
And rivers, full of light and song,
Flash all the flowery vales along ;

And lusty meaders in a row
Rich purple fields of herbage mow ;
And rosy maidens ted the swath
Soft treading on the aftermath,
As age and infancy the while
Lie basking in the summer's smile.

Harborne, June, 1877.

TO THE SOUTH-WEST WIND.

CHILD of the lovely, and the sweet,
  Whose home is like an opal bright,
Where fairest things with fairest meet
  All pure as pearl and lily light;
Thy parents wedded in the spring,
When woods and streams were carolling.

Hail! thou art doubly welcome now;
  For full of turmoil and unrest,
I reverently bare my brow,
  Sweet soother of my ruffled breast;
Breathe thou upon me as of yore,
And bitterness is mine no more.

O why? when Nature's work is pure,
  When beauty is to beauty true,
When apple bud and bloom are sure
  To greet the cluster-rose's hue,
Is man, the master-work of God,
The falsest thing upon the sod?

Truth left the starry region'd skies,
  And came to sojourn among men;
But wounded sore in Paradise,
  She sought her native home again;
When Abel bade her stay awhile,
Till Cain pursued her with his guile.

And ever since in woodland ways,
  A fugitive from man she goes,
To hide **in an** untrodden maze ;
  . **Her breath the odour of** a rose,
Which poets scent, **and in** their strife,
Find the nepenthe of their life.

An angel softly whispering ;
  A spirit of earth's holy **prime,**
With a sweet perfume in her **wing**
  That telleth of another clime,
Where liveth He who loveth all,
With love that did survive the fall.

———

ILFRA.

LITTLE sweet lily-bloom, pearl **of my** love,
  When I first saw her in **raiment of white,**
Fresh from the seraphine **region** above,
  Life was a rapture **and vision** delight.

Bright as the dew, in the meadows of June,
  From the soft azure that circled her eye,
Sparkled **a light,** as she lay at the noon,
  In her babe-wonderment, watching the **sky.**

All that the heart of a poet desires,
   Met in this dear little dot of a toy ;
Gentleness lit with the purest of fires,
   Beauty illum'd with the dimples of joy.

Doubt of a heaven is sin against grace ;
   Look on her features and see how they shine
With an effulgence that filleth the place,
   Purity's nimbus around the divine.

Fairest and sweetest, and brightest and best,
   Ne'er be her Ichabod written, pray we ;
Sad are the hearts with no dove in the nest ;
   Babes make a Paradise ever for me.

December 23, 1879.

EPITHALAMION.

THE BRIDEGROOM TO HIS BRIDE.

Thou peerless jewel of my heart,
   God's crowning gift to me,
My fairer, sweeter, better part,
   What shall I proffer thee ?
Come in and fold thy wings, sweet dove,
   Here peace hath made her nest ;

And love in answer to my love
  Shall dwell within thy breast.
The bird that warbles by the way
  Shall sweeter sing for thee,
And roses blushing on the spray
  Shall richer blow for me.
I feel my happiness complete,
  And naught shall make me roam ;
My pulse of life doth truer beat,
  My heart is now at home.
No more I chide the powers above,
  Lone, weary, and opprest,
For in the sunshine of thy love
  My soul hath found her rest.

CHORUS OF FRIENDS.

Strew the roses, quaff the wine,
  Fill the golden cup of joy,
Let the lily, let the vine,
  And the orange find employ ;
Love is come to Hymen's shrine,
  Strew the roses, quaff the wine.

THE BRIDE TO THE BRIDEGROOM.

I come, I come unto thy call,
  Thy darling and thy bride,
And whatsoever may befall,
  With thee, love, to abide ;

My heart to thine shall ever beat,
  Thy trials let me share,
Then life shall be a dainty sweet,
  And joy my daily fare.
There's not a cloud that passes by
  I will not brighter make,
And if my burthened breast should sigh,
  I'll chide it for thy sake.
My heart is loyal, thou art lord ;
  In thy light let me shine ;
And I, attentive to thy word,
  Will every wish divine.
All the pure homage of thy love
  To me is freely given ;
And thou shalt that devotion prove
  Which makes the home a heaven.

CHORUS OF FRIENDS.

Strew the roses, quaff the wine,
  Fill the golden cup of joy,
Let the lily, let the vine,
  And the orange find employ ;
Love is come to Hymen's shrine,
  Strew the roses, quaff the wine.

October 7th, 1875.

MY LOVE-LAND.

Soft are the winds that kiss the south,
  And bright her sun that shines on high;
A rich carnation is her mouth,
  And blue as April bells her sky;
But softer are the perfumed gales,
  That wanton waft across thy breast,
My homeland, with the pleasant vales,
  Sweet crown and beauty of the West!

'Tis there the wildling of the Spring,
  Is first to peep, and tell the time
For maids to saunter out and sing,
  And lads to woo them in the prime;
And there September oft is seen
  In June's bright raiment gaily drest,
With gardens, groves, and woods a-green,
  For so enchanting is the West.

A land of honey, milk, and cream,
  Whose showers are sweet as roses' tears;
Romantic as a poet's dream,
  And fresh as the primeval years;
A region rich in fairy tales,
  Where happy mortals go in quest
Of rarest joys; such are the vales
  Of my dear love-land in the West.

I've seen our grand historic sights,
　Proud Warwick's hold, and Windsor's towers,
And scenes of old heroic fights,
　And Avon's golden lily flowers,
And heard the charmer, Nilsson, sing—
　A nightingale with throbbing breast—
But all such memories take wing
　Before my home-land in the West.

My sire-land! birth-land! love-land! all
　That makes a minstrel prize his home,
Nurse of my muse, at Spring and Fall,
　And keeper of my fathers' tomb :—
My soul is thine, and treason vile
　It were to say that I am blest,
Save when I bask beneath thy smile,
　My own dear darling of the West.

There maids blush not to show the red
　Rich sign of health upon their cheek ;
And men are never taught to dread
　The honest truth that they should speak ;
And hospitality invites,
　Nor scorns to call the poor man guest,
And all enjoy their native rights,
　As true-born children of the West.

And while I hold, where duties lead,
　That every man should play the brave,

Although they make his heartstrings bleed,
  And promise him a foreign grave—
Yet all supreme are Nature's charms,
  And I, of beauty, am possest ;
So take me, Devon, in thy arms,
  And fold me to thy loving breast.

POLLY PELLEW.

SONG.

My beautiful Lowman ! *
My own native Lowman !
Dear meadowland melody !
  Sweetest of streams !
I would I were near thee,
To see and to hear thee,
And pluck the fair lilies
  That blow in my dreams.
Beside the bright Lowman,
The Beautiful Lowman,
My soft singing Lowman,
  Rose-shaded and blue,
In the light o' the gloaming,
I met in my roaming,
  The pride o' all maidenhood.
    Polly Pellew.

* Pronounced Loman.

My beautiful Lowman !
Sweet willow-kiss'd **Lowman** !
No lilt in love's song,
   Hath such music for me ;
For pearl o' bright waters !
Know Devon's fair daughters,
Grow proud o' their beauty,
   When mirror'd by **thee.**
Yet Lowman ! bright Lowman !
My beautiful **Lowman** !
When sweet with **thy hawthorns.**
   That whiten the **view,**
For love let me ask thee,
In sooth it will task thee,
   Say, what are **thy** charms without
      Polly **Pellew ?**

My beautiful **Lowman** !
Farewell ! my sweet Lowman !
But prithee dear Lowman !
   Tell this to my love—
When chancing to meet her,
" No lark's note is sweeter
Than Polly's ' Good night,'' '
   Pretty Collipriest dove !
And Lowman ! **dear** Lowman !
My far away Lowman !

As sure as thy daisies
   Are dappled with dew:
I'll envy, I'm thinking,
Each sun in his sinking,
   The glance he is getting from
      Polly Pellew.

ON HEARING THE LARK SING IN OCTOBER.

" Is that the meadow-lark I hear?
   It cannot, cannot be ;
The winds are wild, the leaves are sere,
   And bleak and bare the lea.

Yes, yes, it is, I know his voice,
   I heard him in the Spring,
Hark ! how he bids the earth rejoice,
   While mounting on the wing.

I stand reproved, and blush with shame ;
   I'll seek my silent lute,
If he can sing I am to blame
   To be so cold and mute "

Thus sang I as the little lark,
    Went soaring on his way,
And singing passed into a dark
    And stormy cloud of gray.

And then I musing said, "I deem,
    Mistaken in the hour,
He, now awaking from a dream,
    Of odour breeze and flower—

Away has started on the wing,
    And bursting into song,
Found it is better far to sing,
    Than sleep the Winter long."

But oh, the joy ! to hear his note,
    As, sinking with the sun,
It rippled from his merry throat,
    In a melodious run.

His carol o'er, I came away,
    Charmed with his song and glee,
And dotted down the self-same day,
    These simple lines you see.

Somerset Road, Edgbaston,
    October 4th, 1876.

ALWAYS LEAVE SOMETHING LIKE PLEASURE BEHIND

SONG.

I'll sing you a song in my merriest strain
  To a musical setting a peasant may learn,
And mind you remember the happy refrain
  And troll it well out when it comes to your turn.
There is happiness ever around us, and we,
  By looking about, sure a morsel may find;
Make the best of your blessings, my brothers, and see
  You always leave something like pleasure behind.

'Tis the fault of ourselves, and bad living, my boys,
  If we find nought but bitters, and gather no sweets,
If we dwell on our sorrows, forgetting our joys,
  And mope along counting the stones in the streets.
The world is just like what we make it—a curse,
  If we pass by the good, and are wilfully blind;
'But a blessing, if you will consider my verse,
  And always leave something like pleasure behind.

There is bread, and to spare, for your neighbours and
    you,
  And the face of the toiler would oftener shine,
If men were more human, and friendship more true,
  And water had sometimes a dash of the wine.

Don't think of yourselves in your moments of ease,
  And wherever you are, let your manner be kind,
With a heart full **of** sunshine, you ever must please,
  And always leave something like pleasure behind.

December 19th, **1873**.

THE AFTERGLOW.

I STOOD **upon the** highest table-land,
  Of this our old and much-belovéd isle ;
When not a whispering breeze **the** woodlands **fanned,**
  And evening wore her softest, sweetest smile.

And thus I mused, as o'er the tender green
  Of the rich aftermath, swift flew my sight ;
Oh ! how impressive is the twilight scene !
  When, like a withered lily, fades the light.

Who that has seen **the closing** of the day,
  When Autumn rolls her mighty orb **of fire**
O'er slopes empurpled, **down the** westering gray,
  There like a dying ember **to** expire,—

Nor paused to list the pensive red-breast sing
  His plaintive solo, in the wayside thorn ;
As welcome, now, as joyous **notes** of Spring,
  With which the lusty thrush salutes the morn ?

Who that has marked the witchery of the hour,
  The pomp of pageant sweeping through the air,
Whose gorgeous colours shame both bird and flower,
  And mimic seas, and headlands passing fair,—

Nor ceased his watching, till the cloudy peaks,
  Now tinged with amber, now with sober red,
Burned into crimson, leaving golden streaks,
  Until the heavens seemed opened overhead,—

(A sea of glory ! flooding all the sky,
  So mellow, that in bursting on the sight,
The soul drank in its beauty through the eye,
  And straight pulsated with a new delight,)

And has not felt his waning faith increase
  And hailed it, as a foretaste of that life
When in the everlasting realms of peace,
  Far from this region of tempestous strife,—

In holy ministries of love and joy
  Each ransomed spirit shall be truly blest,
And every faculty find meet employ,
  In heaven's own afterglow of perfect rest ?

The Lightwoods, September 29th, 1876.

G

THE NAILERS' PARADISE.

I'VE been as near to heaven this day,
 As here 'tis possible to be,
If heaven is green, as poets say,
 And all things there are bright to see.
Through fields—if Eden boasted such,
 A foolish creature sure was Eve
To crave that apple overmuch,
 Which forced her the blest spot to leave—
Through fields of rich deep meadow grass
 As ever eye did rest upon,
My darling and myself did pass;
 And lanes with wayside homes, and one,
An antique seven-gabled hall,
 With moss and lichen overgrown,
And legends written on the wall,
 In characters of ivy shown,—
Which, trailing, was most eloquent,
 Of sights its olden folk had seen,
On hospitality intent,
 In days that long ago had been;
While ample doorways told a tale
 Of merry doings in the past,
Roast, revel, song, and good old ale;—
 But now the outer gate is fast,

And the huge iron knocker hangs
  All idly rusting, worn and mute,
No more to tell, with thundering clangs,
  Of horseman with his weary brute.

Now rattle, yellow to the eye,
  As cowslip bells in early Spring,
And trefoil intergrown with rye
  We pass'd where insects on the wing
Were dancing to the wild bee's lyre,
  As speeding merrily along
To nooks with campions afire,
  He sang his pretty summer song.
Then, wandering where the speedwell blew,
  And bistort reared its noble head,
And goldenwort broke on the view,
  And mint grew fragrant 'neath the tread,
A brook, the tiniest ever heard,
  Went babbling through the sunny scene;
Just like the warble of a bird
  When hidden in a thicket green.
O ! pleasant 'twas upon its brink,
  Amid the willow-herb to sit,
And mark the wayward thing, and think
  Few sights were lovelier than it,
While o'er our heads the guelder rose
  Sweet-scented, odorous made the noon ;
And valleys steep'd in soft repose
  Were sultry with the breath of June.

It was too warm for larks to soar,
 So they were nestling with their loves ;
But from a wood came evermore,
 The gentle murmur of the doves.
All mute the grasshopper did rest ;
 The flocks lay drowsy in the shade ;
And kine the fragrant herbage prest,
 As 'neath a tree their couch they made ;
While swelling upland met our gaze,
 And sweeter made the charming sight,
Till melted in a grey-blue haze,
 The firwood on the distant height.

Now o'er the stile and through the lane, .
 Where e'en the very soil was sweet,
When, " How like Devon, dear," said Jane,
 " See overhead the branches meet,
And mark that pool with mossy stones,
 And lady ferns and hedges rich ;
This cottage and those sweet hay-trones,
 And wealth of sycamore and wych.
And see the graceful briony
 With red dog roses on each side,
That prince of wildings, too," said she,
 " The bonny foxglove in his pride."
Yet " World's End " was the only name
 By which was known that spot so fair.
As if in scorn 'twas giv'n, O shame !
 Since Heaven's own silence dwelleth there ;

Save when the hammer's busy sound
Is heard throughout the quiet place ;
For thrifty maidens there are found,
All comely, neat, and fair of face,
With minds intent on winning bread
By forging nails, with earnest eyes ;
And when "Good-Bye" we bade, I said
This is the Nailers' Paradise !

June 28th, 1869.

THINKING.

Ou, the weariness of sorrow !
Oh, the grief that lives apart !
Oh, to think of each to-morrow
With a sad and widowed heart,
When each golden dream has faded
And the moments, one by one,
Clothed in sombre weeds, come shaded
With each rising of the sun !

When the smile of joy hath vanished,
And the lid hangs on the eye,
Which tells of bright hopes banished
And the oft-repeated sigh ;

And the thoughts go idly wandering
 To a tear-besodden mound,
Near where a brook, meandering,
 Gives out its sweetest sound.

Sad must be each last long parting,
 When love's tendrils fondly twine,
And the soul, with bitter smarting,
 Questions o'en the Love Divine ;
Yet it promises a meeting
 On a better, brighter shore,
And we almost hear the greeting
 Of the loved ones gone before !

Patience, then, a litttle longer ;
 What the Father does is best ;
Tribulation makes us stronger,
 Fitting us for endless rest.
God is aye a kind concealer ;
 Faith is better far than sight ;
Time, the healer and revealer,
 Makes the darkest trials bright.

EVENTIDE.

There is a charm of soft delight in summer's twilight
    hour ;
Which whispered words will put to flight as blasts will
    strip a flower :
A stillness speech can ne'er define, too exquisite for
    words—
The hush that reigns at evenchime ! before the chant
    of birds.

O ! it is pleasant then to lean upon a meadow stile,
And let a sense of ecstasy the weary soul beguile ;—
As, gazing on the western hills, enrobed in mist we feel,
That there is still a joy unborn for daybreak to
    reveal :—

But while the vision is entranced with sights almost
    divine,
The rich and golden afterglow o'er ruminating kine,—
Where is the soul with skill to sing the music of the
    songs,
That comes in one harmonious trill from merry
    woodland tongues ?

And, spite the rush and rumble of a distant rolling
    train,
Just like the muffled thunder of the vexed and troubled
    main,—
When the long and deep-dull murmurs of the ground
    sea's hollow roar,
Predict the bursting of a storm upon the rocky shore,—

A bonny little throstle is heard above it all,
And cuckoos o'er the valley, that one another call ;
And ouzel, with his solo pitched in a minor key,
Killing care in every bosom with his witching melody.

But what must be the holy hush !—the pause before
    the night—
Away in some far solitude, of green and golden light,
Where the soft sweet plant of silence grows, and Quiet
    in repose,
Sits listening as the happy birds their vesper chantings
    close ?

A SONG OF JOY.

THE earth has still her paradise,
  And a celestial clime,
With groves and unpolluted skies,
  As in her golden prime :

Where all is peaceful as above,
  And brooding turtles sigh,
And croon their tender notes of love
  In fragrant woodlands nigh.

Death triumphs not o'er all below,
  Nor saddens every hour ;
Times are when gales of heaven will blow,
  And joys immortal flower ;

When music soaring to the clouds
  Will on the sunbeam float,
And sing to the enraptured crowds
  With an impassioned note.

Then sounds seraphic fill the air
  As in the balmy June,
When all is beauty everywhere,
  And nature is in tune.

Yes, earth **has** still her paradise
   And a celestial clime,
With groves and unpolluted skies,
   As in her golden prime.

THE MAIDEN MOWER.

O **WELL** **for** the man that marries thee
   With the stout strong heart and hand ;
Let thy scythe ring out right merrily,
And thy step be that of the truly free,
Proud of thy maidenly majesty,
   Thou child of the free-born band.

The mountain air is in each breath
   Thy heaving bosom draws ;
Health's rose on thy cheek aye flourisheth
In spite of the deadly darts of death.
" So shall it be," dear nature saith,
   " Where they obey my laws."

Fair as a pearl, and undefiled,
   No town-stained spoil art thou,
But pure as is the little **child**,
Whose fellowship is with the wild,
I see thee there a presence mild,
   All peace and worship now.

THE POET'S HOMILY.

Ye doubters of a power divine,
  I pray you halt awhile with me ;
Those brionies that ever twine,
These honied clarions **of** the bine,
  This little reverent lily see.

How lived they when **the** wintry snow
  Lay white upon **the** dreary land ;
When northern winds did biting blow,
When noon-suns, **too,** had failed **to glow,**
  And ice-rocks strewed the frozen **strand ?**

You answer, " There are potent **laws,"**
  I grant, my friends, that such there be :
Still there's the flower, we need a cause ;
Whence came its beauty, whence, I pause—
  If not from the Divinity ?

I'll tell you who adorned the rose,
  With crimson robes and made it sweet ;
One morn, when men from their repose
Stirred not, though tears of orphans' froze
  O'er mothers in their winding sheet,

A gentle spirit came this way ;
  No matter whence, or what his name,
And here invisible did stay
The tiny bantling to array,
  And lit it with a living flame.

You smile,—when you can chain the springs,
  The truth of this you then may doubt ;—
Know often in my wanderings
I hear the rush of unseen wings,
  And looking find the flowers are out.

I AM THINKING, LOVE, OF THEE.

SONG.

I am thinking, love, of thee,
  My Janie dear,
While the tears are falling free,
  My Janie dear,
I am thinking when I'm gone,
Few will care for thee or none,
For the world unto the lone
  Is so cold, my dear.

I am thinking of thy worth,
  My Janie dear,
My pride of all the earth,
  Sweet Janie dear,

And the patience that could bear,
With my failings and my care,
And thy laugh at old despair,
  My Janie dear.

I have sometimes seen thee weep,
  My Janie dear,
When the trial was not deep,
  My Janie dear,
But when others wore a frown,
As fair fortune's star went down,
Then no wife in all the town,
  Was like thee, my dear.

If a moment thou wert vexed,
  My Janie dear,
I have seen thee smile the next,
  My Janie dear,
For a kiss I gave to thee,
Love's seal of sympathy;
But a thought now troubles me,
  My Janie dear.

There is one outside the door,
  My Janie dear,
Who spares nor rich nor poor,
  My Janie dear,

He waves a shadowy wand
As I look out on the land,
Then he beckons with his hand,
  My Janie dear.

I must lay me down and sleep,
  My Janie dear,
And this word I pray thee keep,
  My Janie dear,
Place my hands across my breast,
And bear me to the west,
Where our belovéd rest,
  My Janie dear.

It pains me to the heart,
  My Janie dear,
To think that we must part,
  My Janie dear;
But one must go before,
So prithee grieve no more :
Death hath its sunny shore :
  My Janie dear.

THE LITTLE MISCHIEF MAKER.

'Twas bonny Midsummer, bright noon of the year,
  The amorous Earth lay wooing the sky,
  Soft fanned by the zephyrs that busy flew by,
Each whispering love-stories into her ear.

The air was ambrosia, life was delight,
  The roses were faint with the sweet breath of June,
  The cushat chimed in with the merry merle's tune,
And the day was so long that it banished the night.

When thus to young Love rosy Pleasure began,
  " Wilt go to yon greenwood and revel awhile?"
  " By all means," said he with the pleasantest smile,
And scampered away to the haunts of old Pan.

On where the heather-bell bends with the bee ;
  On where the billberry purples the brake ;
  Over the mossy turf they their way take,
Wild as the deer, in the height of their glee.

On where the gorse-covered hillocks are seen
  Dotting the downs with the sunniest glow,
  Whilst hither and thither a rich overflow
Of fresh ferny beauty enlivens the green.

"Halt !" shouted Pleasure ; "And wherefore ? " asked
   Love ;
"Look yonder, look, what a beautiful maid !"
"Nay, nay," answered Cupid, "for I am afraid
You ill brook a rival, you beauties above."

Then holding his little bow over his eyes,
   To shield them awhile from the gaze of the sun,
   He rent the still air with his boisterous fun,
Which took pretty Pleasure, poor thing, by surprise.

"I think I will aim at those cherries," quoth he,
   And he pointed away o'er the heather, "Oh dear !
   I never saw lips half so ruddy appear,
You never would shoot at mere cherries," said she.

"Well, then, at that stately young lily I saw,
   When first to the spot you directed my sight."
  "You never met lily, you urchin, so white ;
Your shaft for a lily you never would draw."

"I'll aim at those pretty twin violets blue."
  "Oh, plague me no more with your nonsense, my
   boy,
  No violets ever could give you such joy,
Though fed with the daintiest honey and dew."

"Shall I shoot at that blush-rose?" "O mischievous
    deed !
  That sweetens not only the air, but my eyes,
  Hush, hush, you young scoundrel, for I am too wise ;
The heart of another fair victim must bleed."

Ta-wang ! went the string of his bow, and the sound
  Made Pleasure start back with affright in the rear ;
  Then the damsel she saw, through a pitiful tear,
With her hand on her bosom half dead from a wound.

"Fie fie, Love," said Pleasure, "how wrathful I feel !
  How, how could you, boy, that young innocent harm?"
  "Know, Pleasure," spake he, "I bear with me a charm
The wound that I make I can evermore heal."

When, lo ! from a nook in the forest-side near,
  And hard by a rill, which a melody ran,
  A youth, with the state of a neighbouring swan,
Came bearing along like the king of the mere.

And passing the maiden he stopped to inquire
  What meant the confusion he saw in her eyes,
  And if she was hurt, and what of her sighs,
Those winds with which Cupid was fanning his fire.

When thus Ethelina—for so she was named :
  "A man in the forest I saw, when my heart
  Was struck, as it were, with the barb of a dart."
Quoth he, "It was Love," and the wicked boy blamed :

  I

And kissing the beauty—Love's solace for pain—
" There, there," chuckled Cupid, **" see Pleasure, she
　　smiles."**
" Away," answered Pleasure, " I see by your wiles,
The hearts that you break are soon mended **again."** `

　　Cannock Chase, **1886.**

WEE-MAGGIE.

THE latest of **a lovely** group,
That make a charming band,
I hailed her advent, **at her birth,**
Upon life's sunny **strand.**

" Another pretty sweetling born,"
I said, with sudden glee ;
" A little smiling seraph sent
With holy ministry."

And yet there **was** a feeling, too,
Of sadness reigned around,
Which gave a pathos to the **mirth,**
That everywhere was **found.**　.

For who could tell the destiny,
Which did that babe await ?
The pain, perchance the agony,
Now meted out by fate.

So thought I, as upon my **way,**
To hear the throstle sing,
A gleam of glory crossed my **path,**
More beautiful than spring.

A little pair of sunny cheeks,
With just a tender flush,
Of pearl and rose-pink, interfused,
Too delicate to blush.

And softer than the vernal beam,
Seen in **an** April **sky,**
The light her glance **of** Heaven had caught,
Shone captive **in her eye.**

It was a vision **of delight,**
And blessing God above,
I kissed it as **His** latest gift,
Of what the angels love.

Harborne, May 30th, 1880.

THE COUNTRY SQUIRE.

SONG.

A RIGHT merry man was the country Squire,
  That liv'd in days of old ;
When the little dog turn'd the spit by the fire,
Till the haunch was done to his heart's desire ;
And his daughters sat with the village quire,
  The lambs of his cosy fold.
And many a toast had the good old host,
  As he gather'd his neighbours round,
Here's one—" A heart for charity,
Who gives to the poor, right blest is he,"
So honour your horn, and drink with me,
  To its sentiment, true and sound.

The pride of his soul, was a noble hall,
  With ample hearth and door ;
Where all who pass'd were wont to call,
And never a guest was heard to brawl :—
For he had a cheery word for all,
  The rich man and the poor.
Another good toast of the blithe old host,
  As he gather'd his neighbours round,—
" The man that learns from the busy bee
To sweeten the fruit of industry."
So honour your horn, and drink with me,
  To the health of a man so sound.

In the glorious days of good Queen Bess,
   His grand old house was rear'd ;
Where ancient elms with a fond caress,
Bent over its roof, as if to bless
The inmates in their happiness,
   As the rooks sang wild and weird,
To the hearty toast of the good old host,
   As he gather'd his neighbours round ;
" Who lives to himself, a fool is he,
Of the very first, and last degree."
So honour your horn, and drink with me,
   'Tis a sensible toast, and sound.

Of bountiful heart, and generous hand,
   His laugh was loud and long ;
And to hear him sing, the anthem grand,
As reverent he, in church would stand,
Mellowing all the vocal band,
   Was to hear the soul of song.
But he is gone ; and under a stone
   He sleeps the sleep profound :—
So let us drink to his memory,—
A nobleman of the first degree ;
Whose good name evermore shall be,
   A sweet and pleasant sound.

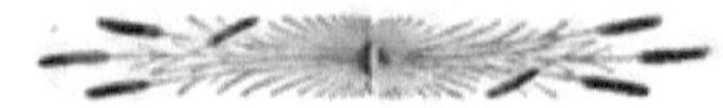

FIND A WAY, OR MAKE IT.

A STORY in heroic rhyme of valour and its meed,
And how a life was made sublime by an immortal deed !
There was a castle on a hill, with moat to bar the way,
So strong **that** ten had kept **at** will an arméd **host**
    at bay ;
And many **a valiant** **son of** Mars had braved the gory
    steep,
Whose fate was to return **with scars, and fly the**
    frowning keep :—
At length a doughty **warrior came, and** sitting **down**
    before it,
Resolved his sword should carve his name **on** the grim
    hold—and swore **it.**

Then winding **loud** his battle-horn, thus spake he to
    his band,—
Be **ready on** the morrow-morn, with trusty blade in
    hand ;
Those **castellated** battlements that **proudly pierce the**
    sky,
The fury **of** the elements no longer shall defy :
That flag, **see,** flaunting in the sun, above the **fortress**
    walls,
But kindly waves to woo us on, and beckons, **not**
    appals :—

" Up, braves ! 'tis yours "—With might and main they
    strove, but failed to **take** it ;
When " Follow me," he cried again, " I'll *find* **a way,**
    or MAKE it."

Quick clearing the deep **moat and** gorge, and rushing
    up the slope,
Straight as a bolt from **Vulcan's forge, all** courage,
    heart, **and** hope,
He with them, **over** toppling **crags, and huge** impeding
    blocks,
Soon reached **the** fort, like **winded** stags when hunted
    over rocks ;
There, spite **the** hissing **shot, and flood of** burning
    molten **lead,**
And blindness **from the** gush of blood that trickled
    down **each** head,
They clung to " The Impregnable," **till they could**
    hardly brook **it,**
While, with a will invincible, he *cut* his way and TOOK
    it.

So when the soul upon a thing is set, and it is right,
Let Resolution be the king, and leader in the fight !
And if this truth be understood, that on life's battle
    plain,
Kind heaven is ever with the good to succour and
    sustain,

That though the struggle may be **hard,** and fortitude
    be tried,
All efforts meet with due reward, when on a **righteous**
    side,
We shall heroically pursue our course, when **we begin**
    it ;
And **keeping** aye the goal in view, **press on, and nobly**
    WIN it.

THE TWINS.

Ivy and Holly are two little pearls ;—
    Two pretty jewels to string on my line ;
Two little sunny-faced seraph-like girls,
    Sweet little treasures, I would they were mine.

Mine, for the sake of the beauty they bring ;
    Mine, for the love in their innocent **eyes ;**
Mine, for the casket of songs I would sing ;
    Mine, for the message **they** bear to the wise.

List ! the glad tidings they preach to the earth :
    " Beauty and joy for your winterly hours ;
Lift up your hearts with thanksgiving and mirth,
    Life were a wilderness but for the flowers."

PRIMROSES AND VIOLETS.

PRIMROSES and violets
   All the way from Devon !
Pretty floral prophecies
   Of a future heaven.

Gathered by a sister's hand,
   In the mossy nooks
Of our pleasant hawthorn-lanes,
   By the waterbrooks.

Little lowly folk are they,
   Yet I often dream,
That I see a saintly face,
   Mid their blossoms gleam.

And methinks that even **now,**
   As I view their **charms,**
I can see my pretty babe
   Folded in my **arms.**

So I send the giver thanks,
   Perfumed with my love,
For her pretty prophecies,
   Of the world above.

VICTOR.

A PORTRAIT.

WITH true prevision which foresaw
  The task my willing muse essays,
They nam'd him Victor, but I'll draw
  This little Puck among the fays.

He shall not snuff my purpose out :
  Behold the sunny elf of earth,
So full of laughter, love, and shout,
  That every maiden calls him Mirth.

Cap-crown'd and bluff as Hal or Jack,
  In a sea-jerkin there he stands,
Broad-shoulder'd with a burly back,
  And dark hose ring'd with scarlet bands.

A sturdy little Briton bold,
  With round cheeks shining like the morn,
Red, plump and set in shocks of gold,
  Like poppies in the yellow corn.

To see his gleaming eyes of blue,
  Flash out their living lights o' fire,
Like sapphires in the early dew,
  Is just to have your heart's desire.

Then there's a music in his voice,
  As free as that the throstle sings,
A sound to make the soul rejoice,
  And give the weary spirit wings.

Fresh from the land of Innocence,
  And glowing with cherubic love,
He brings with him an affluence,
  Of purity and joy above.

And yet he is so human, too,
  So roguish, rollicking, and quaint,
And jaunty, if I must be true,
  He's nine o' Cupid three o' saint.

Thus without knowing it, he bears
  Himself in such a gallant way,
That when he his Glengarry wears,
  He makes the girls an easy prey.

He smiles and they return his smile,
  Until it comes to a caress,
When lo! he steals, with artless wile,
  Their hearts, but not their happiness.

And when he greets you at the door,
  And sings his pretty welcome in,
A giant Cormoran o' four,
  With Joy's own dimple on his chin.

Heart-whole his little chubby hand,
   He offers in so frank a way,
You own him **chief** of all **the band,**
   Whose bliss it is to eat and **play.**

My sketch is done, and **I'm in tears,**
   For life is not unmingled joy,
I think me of the future years,
   And tremble **for the happy boy.**

But God is **good** the **while I** weep,
   The Summer-time will have its **showers,**
And he who gave knows **how to keep**
   This treasure of our earthly **bowers.**

A SPRING PSALM.

" SWEET primal season, effluence **divine** !
   Thou bright perennial from the fields of life,
Make earth once more thy consecrated **shrine,**
   And hush the tumult of tempestuous strife.

Come, as of old, with vivifying breath,
   Pearl, blue, and silver, sunny sky, and cloud,
And Beauty, springing from the bed of death,
   Shall break the trammels of her icy shroud."

The hills are touched, and lo! their summits smoke ;
  The sea-fowl seek again their native strand ;
The hawthorns redden underneath the oak ;
  Broad rivers laugh, and greener grows the land.

Deep in the dell the wild bee's harp is heard ;
  High in the azure Heaven's own minstrel sings ;
Impassioned music fires the forest bird,
  While tremulous raptures vibrate in his wings.

The flowers are all devotion ; Nature's nun
  In snow-veil drops her head in silent prayer ;
With conscious joy the crocus greets the sun,
  And fragrant with thanksgiving is the air.

A holier impulse stirs in every soul,
  With each new revelation from above ;
Thou Spring, art one, we yield to thy control,
  And hear creation whisper, "God is Love."

HOMELY COUNSEL.

Never mind the little "trifles,"
  Fraying from the robe of life,
Make not troubles out of trifles,
  They come fast enough, my wife.

THE TRYST.

A PICTURE of a bygone time,*
  My faithful pen would draw,—
Bright summer at the morning-chime,
  Beside **the** silver Taw.

A long straight line of dusty way,
  A mile, may be, or more ; †
With just a little gentle play,
  Of shadow passing o'er.

A soft, suffused, and pearly glare
  Of dreamy light **on** high ;
Which breaking, lit a face as fair,
  As ever saw the sky.

A tender tremor in *her* heart,
  Of ecstasy acute;
Which plays a more intensive part,
  As *he* is nearing, mute.

And yet no sailor longed for day,
  More than the **two to** meet;
But this is Love's delightful way,
  Of making trysting sweet.

---

* 1839. † On the Braunton Road, Barum.

THE PLAYGROUND.

THE thing impossible to some,
    To others is an easy feat ;
An obstacle to overcome ;
    A difficulty made to beat.

Your genius is a clever wight—
    Prometheus-like he stands alone
And stops the levin in its flight,
    To play upon a telephone.

But when he paints the imp of fun,
    Besmear'd with cream and mazard-pie,
Or taps the rain-cloud with a gun,
    Or hangs it on a line to dry—

I'll own that then there'll be a chance,
    For one to catch the subtle charms
Of urchins, in the playful dance,
    Of their mercurial legs and arms.

Still he who dares to throw the ball,
    May tumble o'er a pin or two ;
And perseverance conquers all—
    So, I'll just try the thing to do.

The rough-and-tumble-romp and glee,
   Of children bounding out of school ;
Or dance around a wishing-tree,
   Beat all the May-games of the Fool.

What merry antics children play !
   What funny figures they will make !
And what delightful things they say,
   Of their capacities for cake.

But **let** me sketch them, as about
   They writhe, or wriggle, here and there';
Now victors bold, **now put to rout ;**
   Sec ! now they run "The Racing Mare.'

Well done ! that's right ! around again !
   And I'll be of your merry band,
O never mind a drop o' rain,
   'Twill freshen much the droughty land.

Now, one, two, three, and off you go ;
   Hurrah ! the little fellow wins :—
Tho school-bell rings, 'tis always so !
   They've done before a man begins.

DREAM THOUGHTS.*

From common objects wholesome truths we learn.
Observe those hedgerows in their wanton sport,
Winding and intersecting on their way,
Dividing now, and now uniting—thus
The common boundaries, and the links of all :—
So, too, with the relationships of men ;
Thus far, in common sympathy we run—
And in our public duties intermix,
When, lo, the limit of our social state
Is bounded by the private liberties ;—
Which, each respecting, make the commonweal.
Behold ! again, how the defensive thorn
Wears all his spiky armour as on guard,
To hold his own, and keep intruders off ;—
While, yonder, in a pretty interchange
Of pleasant courtesies, the vetch and rose
Are fondling with the honeysuckle : so,
Learn we where our common interest lies,
By seeking, for the general happiness,
The use, delight, and harmony of all.

---

* A curiosity, composed one night by the Author in his
sleep, and written down the next morning.

I

SHADOWLAND.

Alone ! in the silvery sunshine,
   That lit my quiet bower ;
Watching the bright clouds flitting
   Over a golden flower,—
I mused upon the bygone,
   And waving fancy's wand,
It brought back many a vision,
   From Memory's shadowland.

Now came with soft eyes pleading,
   A dear familiar face !
With **the** sweet smile **of an** angel,
   That beamed with love and grace ;
And I knew by **her** gentle footfall,
   Like snow upon the **sand**—
'Twas the long-lost **form** of my mother,
   From the deep-dark shadowland.

Then, one in **the pride of manhood,**
   Passed **on** before my sight,
With the stately step and bearing
   Of a true and gentle knight :
And tenderly smiled, as fondly
   He beckoned with his hand,
That **I** knew it could be none other
   Than my love, from the shadowland

So with joy beyond all measure,
  I seek my pleasant bower ;
For I see in each fair cloud passing,
  Over that lonely flower,
A sign that the links now broken,
  In our once happy band—
Shall soon be again united
  In a brighter, holier land.

TO CECILIA.

Who that has read thy countenance aright,
  And has not found a poem in each feature ?
Bright, sparkling eyes, rich fountains of delight,
  And brow, the mirror of some happy creature,
Reflecting the effulgence of a clime
Far from the ravages of woe and time.

A dainty clarion is thy rosy mouth,
  Whence issue notes, that evermore are bringing
Sweet memories of the soft and sylvan South,
  Where meadow-larks with meadow-brooks are sing-
    ing ;
Whose laugh is a delicious melody,
Like rippled music of a summer-sea.

But who can paint the blushes on thy cheeks !
  In their own radiant sunshine, ever glowing ;
Where innocence to hide a covert seeks
  Like golden beetle, in the red rose blowing ;
And mirth's sweet dimple where young Joy repairs,
Love's pretty playground, when our heart he snares.

And then thy mien ! with what an easy grace,
  Thy head is borne, e'en envy's self disarming ;
As noiselessly thou glid'st from place to place,
  Thy native elegance our vision charming :
In fine the poet would distracted go,
Were every damsel to enchant him so !

PIXY-LAND.

THE Pixies are a happy band,
  And live right merrily,
And only in a pleasant land
  Are they content to be.
Hence, oft their footprints may be seen
  Around Weargifford Hall ;—
For there the little folk in green
  Will hold their festival.
And those familiar with their ways,
  And pretty elfin tricks,

In June may see the merry fays
  With fiddlers fifty-six,
And often find their parasols
  Left on the fairy green,
Brought there from sunny primrose knolls
  In Pixy Copses seen.
Down in yon meadow by the stream,
  The dapper folk resort;
And while we weary mortals dream
  They 'hold their royal court.
Blithe Killcare is the pixy King;
  Fair Brighteye is his Queen;
And round them on a mushroom ring
  Their aristocs are seen.
Some, quaffing from sweet lily bells
  Deep draughts of honey dew;
And others working mischief-spells
  In evil hoods o' blue.
And one on a bright dragonfly
  Is riding, the bold knight
Of little Goldenwing, the shy,
  His love and sole delight.

*   *   *   *

Now tripping o'er the shaven green,
  A host of ladies go,
Attending on the pixy Queen,
  A right brave royal show,—

Safe guarded by a thousand **fays,**
　All bearing thistle-spears,
With plumes of kingfishers and jays,
　And moorhens, on **the** meres,
To deck their helmets, which are made
　Of golden beetles' wings ;
And, **for a** dirk, each **has** a blade
　Of swordgrass from the springs.
And now the herald blows amain
　His honeysuckle horn,
To summon all the fairy **train**
　To feast before **the morn :**
When to an islet **up the** wave
　The merry elves repair ;
King, Queen, bold knight and baron brave,
　And lovely ladies fair.
Where by a glowworm's tiny light,
　Upon a mossy floor,
For table, stands a mushroom **white**
　Midst pixy stools, a store ;
With silvery lichens for their plate,
　And golden ones also,
And daisy dishes laid in **state**
　With mint and **minnow's roe.**
There, having feasted full and well
　Within their fairy bower,
They sip rose-nectar from a shell
　Until the dawning **hour ;**

When Robin Goodfellow drops in,
  And Puck with his halloo,
And Plague o' Dreams, as owls begin
  To hoot their weird tuwhoo.
At which the merry fiddlers play
  Their last tune for the night,
And dancing merrily away
  All vanish out o' sight.
When soon is heard the cuckoo's rote,
  And then the blackbird's song,
And then the skylark's merry note,
  And next the thrush's tongue ;
But maids out ere the sun doth rise
  That morn are pixy-led,
While many a little changling lies
  A stranger to its bed.

TO MR. JOHN MORRISON.

ON HIS PRESENTING THE AUTHOR WITH TANNOCK'S
AUTOTYPE PORTRAIT OF ROBERT BURNS.

Dear Jock ! I think you will allow
That, as a rule, I might avow,
My grateful tongue finds words enow,
        To thank a friend :—

But faith! I've had to rub my crown,
And pace my study up and down,
Just like a sorely puzzled clown,—
                    From end to end,

'Ere I could get my thoughts to rhyme;
Yet perseverance wins in time,
And so about the curfew chime,
                    A few more turns
Gave me the impulse that I lack'd:
And since my purpose never slack'd,
My muse refusing to be hack'd,
                    Caught sight o' Burns!

There was he hanging on my wall—
Coat, breeks, and gaiters, hat and all;
With papers for a random scrawl
                    O' happy thought;
And faithful Luath by his side,
Intently watching, open-eye'd,
As if the fancy he espied,
                    Which Rab had sought.

Behind, the kirk o' Alloway,
Which made him sing the eerie lay
Of Tam O' Shanter's drunken fray,
                    Was standing lone;

With just a bonny blink o' sky,
To woo the poet's wandering eye,
Soft stealing through the window by,
   From Dian's throne.

Oh ! **what a grand** and stalwart form !
Just made to brave the wildest storm !
And yet to spare the crawling worm
   His tender **heart,**
Like Cowper's, oft would **prompt his foot**
To pass the reptile by the root ;
Or watch **it,** 'mid his choicest fruit
   Enjoy its part.

'Twas in my later youth I met
The lays of Scotland's darling pet ;
But never Jock shall I forget,
   When first I heard
" Ye Banks and Braes," and "Auld Lang Syne,"
And that proud favourite of mine,
" **A** Man's a **Man,**" each **fervid line**
   My nature stirred.

And if a ploughman so can write,
And yield his fellows such delight !
" **I'll try a hand,** for truth and right,
   And sing a song,"

I said ; and Jock thou well dost know,
How I have sought to lessen woe,
And make the darkness brighter glow,
   And smote the wrong ;

When, too, I fail'd to hit the strain,
To soothe a fellow-creature's pain,
A gentle hint from thee again,
   Would set me going ;—
And now thy gift o' Burns inspires,
The dying sparks o' latent fires,
Which kindling yearns with great desires,
   For better doing.

So if I find my courage flag,
And Pegasus behind to lag,
Or, life move with a heavy drag,
   Mine eyes I'll raise
To him, who sang of Liberty,
Love, Nature, and Humanity ;
And doing nobler work through thee,
   Win nobler praise.

Harborne, October, 22nd. 1877.

A FLORAL FANCY.

SWEET flowers, how many parts ye play,
    In the old mystery of Love !
And were we wise in what you say,
    More we might know of things above.

God has no loveless solitudes,
    Howe'er remote the heavenly sphere ;
Nor shade where Indolence intrudes,
    Or Pity vainly drops her tear.

And so I dream and half believe
    The blossoms of this lovely land,
Their souls of incense may receive
    From the benignant angel-band.

And that in yonder realms of light
    There are who choose the buds to tend,
And unseen in their joyous flight
    Do hitherward their journey wend.

First seeking out the rosy queen
    To place their censers on her throne,
Next hieing with a smile serene
    To greet the lily, chaste and lone.

Then, where Love-lies-a-bleeding, shed
  Their rich aroma o'er the spot,
Till making odorous his bed
  With heartsease and forget-me-not.

O ! sweet to think e'en angels feel
  A pleasure in such fond employ ;
And sweet the faith that flowers reveal
  This holy ministry of joy.

————

DEAN ALFORD.

The Midsummer sun in his splendour
  Will oft be obscured by a cloud ;
The monarch new-crowned in his palace
  Will put off his robe for a shroud ;
The bird at the height of his warble
  Will often drop dead from the spray
And worth from its summit of glory,—
  And thus it has happened to day.

It is not so much for thy courage,
  Though that of a champion was thine ;
Nor is it because of thy honours
  Philosopher, Poet, Divine ;

Nor is it that thou wert so saintly,
  Our vigils we mournfully keep ;
But because of thy bountiful nature,
  We think of thee missing, and weep.

Sweet teacher, so **wise** and so winning,
  So generous, gentle and true,
So with us, yet gone like the shadows
  Before we could utter adieu,
O ! Master, for ever **departed,**
  Alas ! with thy people **cry we ;**
Yet Heaven's bright casket **of** jewels,
  Must be all the **richer for thee.**

THE MAGDALEN.

O Christ ! I would be wholly Thine,
  A captive of Thy love ;
I yearn to taste the bliss divine
  Thy saints enjoy above.

Thy name beyond all other names
  Hath an enchanting sound,
Which evermore my heart inflames
  And makes my spirit bound.

And yet I worship at Thy gate
  Upon the lowest stair;
An alien to that happy state
  Which Thou wouldst have me share.

I feel Thee near, I touch Thy hand,
  But cannot see Thy face;
Why thus a stranger do I stand
  To Thine abounding grace?

Draw thou a little nearer, Lord,
  That I Thy smile may see;
Would I could take Thee at Thy word,
  And trust alone in Thee.

AN OLD HOME.

THERE is a charm about an old-world scene
  Which softens the asperities of life!
How peaceful all, how sacred, how serene,
  And wide the contrast to the chafe and strife
Of cities, where the bustling, hustling rush
Drives thousands on to perish in the crush.

Just gaze you here, ye hunters after wealth,
  Until the sunshine, filtering through the air

Lights on your spirit, giving joyous health
  To all your being, making foul things fair ;
Believe me, there's a poison in the gain
Which bringeth its possessor after-pain.

I'd rather be the pool, reflecting light
  From yonder morning clouds that roll on high,
And imaging that windmill at the night,
  When the white moon reigns sovereign of the sky,
Than the chained slave of greed, and herd with those
Who never find, till in the grave, repose.

Here, where the very beasts are looking blest,
  Ambition knows no fierce consuming fire ;
The folk have Sabbath alway, peace and rest,
  Since prudence holds the curb on their desire :
While daily duties find them sweet employ,
And simplest pleasures yield continual joy.

Then comes the crowning day of all the seven,
  Blessing the silence of their ancient ways,
When men go up unto the gates of Heaven
  And offer their sweet sacrifice of praise,
Until they feel the Earth is but a stone
From which to step to the Eternal's throne.

OUR GATHERED LAMBS.

The land was parched, and the herbage bare,
   Where a river ran strong and wide,
With the pasture sweet, and the prospect fair,
   Away on **the** farther side ;
While many a lamb, with plaintive **bleat,**
Lay panting at the shepherd's feet.

Faint, famished, sore, **and** travel-worn,
   His helpless charge **the** shepherd eyes,
And some will perish **before** the morn :
   So, ere the fading sunlight **dies,**
Over the water they straight must pass ;
And feed awhile on the meadow-grass.

He knows the love **of the** mother's heart,
   As timorous they trembling stand,
And tenderly performs his part,
   As fondly, with **his** gentle hand,
He gathers a youngling here and there,
And bears it o'er with jealous care.

What though the river be dark **and** deep,
   And swift **and wild** the turgid flood,
Soon hurry o'er the parent sheep,
   Thorn-pierced, and dripping with their blood ;
When every little one that cried
Is laid down by the mother's side.

So Christ, to draw **our** hearts above,
   Oft takes the sucklings to us given,
That **we** might follow **with** our love,
   And meet our missing lambs in heaven ;
When, oh, the joy what **tongue can** tell ?
   Our Shepherd doeth all things well.

SNOW ON THE GRAVES.

How fair and beautiful is snow !
   As silently it falls
On all impurities below,
   In flakes like little palls.

Alas ! that **the polluting foot**
   Its whiteness **should** defile :
But then the sun must **warm the root,**
   To make the landscape **smile.**

How eloquently it doth speak
   Of that celestial shore,—
Where dwell the gentle and the meek,
   And evil reigns no more.

K

Of life's brief term, too, it doth preach,
　　When melting at a breath ;
But here each feather seems to teach
　　The sanctity of death.

Harborne Churchyard, February 27th, 1879.

LILIAN.

A LITTLE spring-bud fair and sweet,
　　That breaks in beauty on our sight ;
Just like the daisy at our feet—
　　A sunny picture of delight.

In love with all things having life,
　　Grass, bee, bird, butterfly and flower,
She plays the part of little wife,
　　And bids them welcome to her bower.

And O ! to hear her baby talk,
　　As by herself she sits and dreams :
" Yes, I will take oo for a walk,
　　And show oo all the woods and streams,

And daisy-fields and colly-boo,
　　And bow-wow, gee-gee, and the baa ;
And oo shall ride the puff-puff, too,
　　And go and see oo ganma, tha ! "

Sweet petsie-pet, and timorous dove,
    Alas ! that all should end in ache ;
Methinks she speaks like one above,
    And fear is *doubled* for *her* sake.

TO JANIE, ON HER BIRTHDAY.

THE plough **was keeping holiday**
    Beneath a drift of sparkling snow,
Where many a green and **glossy** spray,
    With scarlet berries **all** aglow
Gleamed **on the ice-locked water-way,**
    Where erst the purling **rill did flow.**

Bright Jupiter with mystic moons
    Resplendent caught the gazer's sight,
As through **the cold** nocturnal **noons**
    Fair Dian **held her** silver light ;
And March **his wildest Northern runes**
    Shrieked in the sable ear of Night !

Our floral firstling **of the year,**
    Dwarf mother of the **nuts to be,**
Blushed crimson where **the** catkins near
    Hung dangling from the hazel-tree ;
And Nature with her frozen tear,
    The snowdrop, sought the wintry lea.

That tiny pointed shaft of gold,
  The crocus shot from underneath ;
Gay meadow daffodils were bold ;
  The broom was greening on the heath ;
And lambs leapt gamboling from the fold
  Which Spring to Spring do aye bequeath.

Sweet primrose, delicately shy,
  As timorous as maiden-love,
With saintly meekness in her eye,
  And all the softness of the dove,
Bloomed with that golden chalice by,
  Which fabled Hebe bore above.

Then Venus, to illume the earth,
  Bade Mars with her his radiance lend ;
And give thee welcome at thy birth,
  And be thy guardian and thy friend ;
So take my gem of priceless worth,
  Whose value none can comprehend,—

Thy minstrel's homage in the rhyme
  That sings the day when thou wert born ;
When Earth was in her hardy prime ;
  When buds were bursting on the thorn ;
While larks essayed their flights sublime,
  To render jubilant the morn.

March 31st, 1873.

THE THRESHER.

SONG.

THUMP, thump, thump, thump,
  Out upon the wintry gale :
Flump, flump, flump, flump,
  Rings the sturdy thresher's flail.
In the middle of the barn,
  Round his head the threshel goes,
While old Goody spins her yarn,
  In the cottage by the close ;
Thump, thump, thump, thump,
  Out upon the wintry gale,
Flump, flump, flump, flump,
  Rings the sturdy thresher's flail.

Not a minute may he waste,
  He has got his task to do ;
Time speeds on, and he must haste,
  And the light grows dimmer, too ;
Thump, thump, thump, thump,
  Out upon the wintry gale ;
Flump, flump, flump, flump,
  Rings the sturdy thresher's flail.

Forty bundles every day,
  "Handsome-bound" of wheaten-straw,
Clean of corn, to stock the bay,
  For each thresher is the law;
Thump, thump, thump, thump,
  Out upon the wintry gale;
Flump, flump, flump, flump,
  Rings the sturdy thresher's flail.

Pleasant in the days of yore,
  'Twas to stand and see him fling
The smooth holly on the floor:
  While the echoes round did ring,
Thump, thump, thump, thump,
  Out upon the wintry gale;
Flump, flump, flump, flump,
  Rings the sturdy thresher's flail.

But let pass a year or so,
  Threshels will be strange enough,
For the engines faster go,
  Though they have to blow and puff,
Puff, puff, puff, puff,
  On the hill and in the vale;
Fluff, fluff, fluff, fluff.
  This will be the steamer's tale;

Thump, thump, thump, thump,
  Out upon the wintry gale ;
Flump, flump, flump, flump,
  Rings **the sturdy** thresher's flail.

LOVE AND BEAUTY.

SONG.

" **HITHER** fly with sunny wings,
  Rosy-dimpled boy ! "
One behind her lattice sings,
  Light of heart as joy,
" Why should Love and **Beauty sever** !
Come with me and dwell for **ever**,"

Nestling on a sunny **breast,**
  Near a beating heart,
Like a dove in downy nest,
  Nevermore to part ;
Now the boy is asking ever,
" Why should Love and Beauty sever ? "

Time in passing saw the bloom
   Beauty's cheek displayed,
Touch'd it and, too soon, the tomb
   Held the lovely maid ;
Still, young Love is singing ever,
" Not e'en death can us dissever ! "

BONNIE JEANNIE ROBERTSON.

SONG.

O' BONNIE Jeannie Robertson !
O' ken ye Jeannie Robertson !
Of a' the flowers by Beauty made,
That court the sun or woo the shade,
There's nane the fairest o' the fair,
Can wi the Hieland lass compare,
The bonnie Jeannie Robertson.

O' bonnie Jeannie Robertson !
The winsome Jeannie Robertson,
She's sweet and caller, as the June,
Wi' temper, like a sang in tune.
And were the day-god bleend awhile,
She'd licht a' Nature wi' her smile,
Wad bonnie Jeannie Robertson.

O' gie me Jeannie Robertson,
The sonsiĕ Jeannie Robertson,
Whose gowden locks are like the rays
Of Simmer's sun, a bonnie bleeze,
And I wad be content to coo,
And she should be my croodlin doo,
The bonnie Jeannie Robertson.

O' wad ye ken the Robertson?
The bonnie Jeannie Robertson,
The purest sapphire is her ee,
Her mou a cherry a' wad pree,
And by her cheekies, rosebud red,—
Had Nature not Perfection wed
Ye'd ne'er hae seen the Robertson.

And she's my jo, the Robertson,
The bonnie Jeannie Robertson !
My lassie wi the lammie's face,
Whose ilka charm's a peerless grace ;
Whose warble's like a wimplin burn ;
And heart a gift nae god'wad spurn,
O bonnie Jeannie Robertson !

TRUE LOVE.

SONG.

TIME graves his wrinkles on thy brow ;
　And snow-white hairs are twining,
Where smiling locks appeared but now,
　With jetty lustre shining ;
And he has paled thy rosy cheeks,
　And bent thy form so slender ;
But hear, for 'tis affection speaks,
　"True love is ever tender."

The weakling is the Mother's care,
　And wins the most attention ;
The suffering she for it will bear,
　Is past all words' invention :
Be this thy solace then on earth—
　"Sweet love it dieth never ;
Love finds, in death, another birth,
　True love, loves on for ever."

GREAT THOUGHTS.

GREAT thoughts, like high tides, lift us up from the slime
And sludge of the world, with its garbage and grime ;
And bear us away, where the soul is as free
And pure as the Guillemot riding the sea.

THE LIGHTWOODS.

THIS is the Lightwoods ! let us rest awhile,
And watch the sun upon the landscape smile.
Survey the prospect, as the vapours sweep
And chase their shadows over plain and steep.
Here the fair village, o' the pleasant brow,
Sweet Harborne stands ; and there illumin'd now,
The rural haunts of Solihull are seen
Salubrious, sylvan, sunny, and serene.
Behold again that vast expanse of blue !
From East to West the scarlet armies view ;
Now stretching from Godiva's town o' spires,
To where o'er Clent their crimson'd chief retires
Between the Wrekin and Great Malvern's head
While Dudley smiles, and Rowley blushes red.

FOR GWENDOLINE.

PRETTY maiden, must I write
On this tablet dainty-white ;
Own'd by such a charming Grace,
Who can the fair thing deface ?
If so, prithee tell me plain
What must be the chosen strain.

Shall I sing a song of mirth,
Shall I celebrate thy birth,
Or of bane shall be my lay?
Pretty maiden, what dost say?
It is thine to give the theme:
Shall it be the maiden's dream?

Yes, I read it in thine eyes;
Yes, I hear it in thy sighs;
Yes, thy every feature speaks,
Dimpled chin and rosy cheeks,
And those lips so full of song,
Though all silent be the tongue.

As thou wilt so let it be,
Pretty Gwendoline, to thee,
And perchance within this book
One to love thee soon may look,
And interpret every thought:
Poets seldom write for nought.

MALVERN.

A SUGGESTION.

If thou a joy ineffable wouldst know—
  And witness Heaven's effulgence overflow
Its pearly banks, and flood the plains below ;
  Wait till the air is sweet with hawthorn-snow —
Then go and stand on lofty Malvern's height,
  And feast thine eyes on that enchanting sight
When, at the trysting of the day and night,
  The West grows golden with the afterglow.

TAMMIE'S TOKEN.

A rose from Lincombe by the sea !
To say that Tammie thinks o' me.
The gales that wanton in the South
Still linger in its dainty mouth,
So odorous, that all the room
Is fragrant with its rich perfume.
Go, get you down to Lover's Dell
For water from the dripping well,
While as some small return that she
Has favoured me all bards above,
I give it in a melody,
The immortality of love,—
As Moore and Milton would have done,
Had they beheld so fair a one.

THE MAIDEN'S DREAM.

'Tis a vision of the May
With a pleasant meadow-way,
Where a hand enclasps a hand,
Links which lovers understand,
And a damsel fair and coy,
Showing love's first flush of joy.

Now a saunter through the vale
Listening to a low-breathed tale,
Though the fitful blushes run
Crimson as the setting sun,
And a pain **is at** the heart
Where the god has shot his dart.

Then the radiance of a face,
Rapture of a fond embrace,
Mute enjoyment of a feeling
Which will never brook concealing,
And that marriage made above,
Soul with soul, and love with love.

TO G. W. R.

You will remember friend this eve !
  When we came sauntering forth,
And saw the young Moon's golden bow
  Lean back against the North.

There was a silence all around
  That made us pause awhile,
As memories of bygone days
  A moment did beguile ;

For underneath a chestnut tree,
  Linked with a sycamore,
Where grassy hillocks met the gaze
  Around St. Peter's door,

There lay a little neighbourhood
  Of men who loved the fair,
And worshipped all things beautiful
  In earth, and sea, and air.

The old grey tower that centuries
  Had braved the storm and blast ;
The lofty elm-grove, and the yews
  Which sombre shadows cast ;

And cabin on the mountain **side,**
　Roofed o'er with moss and fern,
And skiff on the in-coming tide
　Wood, meadow-land, and burn.

Such were the subjects of his brush,
　Who had the master **hand,**
And with his genius did inspire
　The little loving band.

Now mute **and** peacefully **they** rest
　Within their silent homes ;
Cox, Roberts, Baker, Harper, **all**
　Still loyal **in their tombs.**

Harborne Churchyard, May 14th, 1880.

BY THE ROADSIDE.

WOULD that I could for ever feel
　The rapture that to-day
Fired all my being as I gazed
　Upon the lovely May.

Above me where the tender blue
　Clear as a sapphire shone,
The wingèd **clouds flew** lily-white
　Around her summer throne.

While in the zenith, like a crown
  Of pure effulgent fire,
The sun in royal majesty
  My spirit did inspire.

And then to see the fields of gold
  Framed deep with hawthorn bloom !
And chestnut trees with spreading fans
  Sweet scented with perfume !

And list the music of the birds
  In every wood and grove !
And linger there until you felt
  It was a sin to move !

Such **sights and** sounds are a delight,
  And **fraught with** so much bliss,
That he who heeds them not, the soul
  Of life's true joy doth miss.

Harborne Road, May 19th, 1878.

TO MRS. T——

ON HER PRESENTING THE AUTHOR WITH A DRAWING OF LYNTON, NORTH DEVON.

" He hath forgotten us," I heard thee say ;
    Does April's bird forget the tuneful band ?
No, for a season he may cease his lay,
    But he will come again and charm the land.

Thus, though awhile my muse all silent be,
    True gratitude will e'er perform its part ;
I always pay my debts of poesy
    And dare not be a traitor to my heart.

So take our greeting, and, for " Auld Lang Syne "
    Weed out the harsh thought which has taken root,
Since mistletoe and holly-berries twine
    Thy view of Lynton: love's sweet work and fruit.

We hail thy pictured transcript of the West,
    Or rather one of those sweet scenes which we
Did revel in, when swallows made their nest
    Beneath our eaves beside the Severn Sea ;

For fancy treads again each winding road
    To watch the happy folk who saunter there,
As Labour, for a season, drops his load
    And bathes his temples in the balmy air.

How green the upland ! and how wild **the way**
    O'er which the torrent tumbles in its might,
And blue the alder-shaded pools, where play
    Round golden patens **rich** with summer-light.

Then, leaning o'er huge boulders in the stream,
    We see the fronds **of** lady-ferns outspread ;
And now, **as** lovely as a **poet's** dream,
    The seagull waves his white wings overhead.

This paragon **of** beauty **by the** sea,
    Where waves with foam-fans kiss the rocky shore ;
We have **as** ours, sweet **lady,** thanks to thee,
    To love and look upon **for** evermore.

Harborne, New Year's Eve, **1876.**

LOVE'S DIAL.

THE facial peak ! no negatives for me,
    It is the master-feature of my lay ;
And, whether straight or aquiline it be,
    I have a poet's compliment to pay.

One summer season, Cupid, ere the time
    That clocks or watches asked us for a trial,
While humming o'er Apollo's latest rhyme,
    Thought Dian's nose would make a handsome dial.

So seeking a cool umbrage, in the shade
  He found the huntress sporting all alone ;
When, leading her unto a sunny glade,
  He soon espied a pretty moss-clad stone ;

Where, resting **both,** the urchin and the **maid,**
  She gazing most intently on the sky,
He begged **a kiss ;** when thus she pertly **said,**
  " Nay, not until the sun is zenith-high."

Abashed and waiting, **the** impatient **boy** ·
  Lay watching the slow shadow cross **her** face
Till noon was marked, when, rushing off **for** joy,
  He claimed the **boon,** which she bestowed with grace.

———

TO   A   LADY   FRIEND.

ON HER FIFTIETH BIRTHDAY.

FROM **my** sick couch all faint with pain,
I **send my** warmest, friendliest strain ;
  For **know** if aught can e'er inspire
  A minstrel true to strike **his lyre,**
  'Tis found in those two charms of life—
  The Mother dear **and** tender Wife.
  How oft of late have I been taught
  The value of the loving thought,

As she, the glory of my youth,
Has proved her patience, faith and truth !
Unwearied with the wearing day,
My pains she often did allay ;
And when the night came there sat she,
My angel bright of constancy.
No pang that pierced my quivering frame
But seemed to torture her the same ;
No agonizing groan but tore
Her spirit to its inmost core.
If such the love of woman then—
If such her sympathy with pain—
Base is the ingrate who would shrink,
Though tottering on Death's darksome brink,
To tell the world how much we owe
The gentle wife in time of woe.
And of the Mother's holy part,
Much I could sing would touch the heart ;
Mine eyes have seen—God knows—her care
In my own Mother ; in her prayer,
Her soothing word, her earnest look,
And watch that would no challenge brook.
I, too, may tell of *her*, my love,
The Mother of my missing dove.
Madam, I know thy heart too well,
To think that thou would'st break the spell
That makes me sing so sad a lay
On this thy Jubilee—but say

Ar'n't Mothers all the same—if true—
And Jane has dark eyes just like you ;
A fond and tender wife is she ;
So thinks thy husband too of thee ;
And long may **He** who rules in Heaven
Spare us **our** blooming flowers of Devon.
As *Wives,* **may** every year they live
Find us more love and pleasure give ;
As *Mothers,* **may they** live to see
Their children's children climb their **knee ;**
May every year behold them grow
More Christ-like unto **all** below ;
And when our parting hour shall **come**
May Heaven provide **us** each a Home.

January 20th, 1856.

LOVE'S LETTER BOX.

So pretty, though so petulant, and frolicksome as June,
Young Lettie seemed unto my gaze one sweet mirth-
    making noon—
That, when the harvest dance was o'er, I sought the
    maiden's ear,
And thought I something **had** to say, made up of hope
    and fear.

For one whole hour we walked the lanes, save stopping
    by, each stile,
To **view** the sunny landscape round, and **win her**
    lovely smile ;
For one whole hour she nothing spoke to all I had to say,
Save what a happy time she **spent** at Merriden **one day** ;

And of the pleasant **rustle** which the fragrant **hay-**
    trones made,
While sitting **in the** meadow **there** beneath the **hedge-**
    row's shade ;
And of the merry chat she **had** with **one who loved**
    her well,
And spoke of going there **again, some day, if not to**
    dwell.

I **cannot tell you** what **I felt**—'twas something more
    than **pain** ;
It was an **ache about the** heart, **and throbbing of the**
    brain—
At last I caught her **by the hand,** so soft and lily-white,
And looking up into **her face, all rosy-sunrise** light,

I **told** her of a lissom lass with locks of golden hair,
Bright sapphire eyes and **ruby** lips and cheeks with
    dimples rare,
And that I **had** no heart to give to any one on earth,
For she had **it.** " Poor heartless loon," she laughed out
    in her mirth,

" I pity you ; what can I do to mend your hapless state?"
" Say nothing more, dear maid," said I, " about your
      hedge-row mate,
And ere **another week** be passed, send me a line to **say**
If you are willing I should wed my blue-eyed love in May."

" I will," replied the gentle girl, " to ease thy heart, so
      hear !
You know that little hawthorn nook* just round the
      corner, **dear,**
A slight slip **of** the tongue," **she** said, " but never mind
      it ; see,
There you to-morrow morn **shall** find a letter love, from
      me."

With that she gave **a chuckle,** like the **blackbird's joyous**
      crow,
And **flitted like a fairy in** the golden afterglow,
And oh ! I felt so lonely, and **a twelvemonth** seemed
      that night,
But at daybreak I was waking with a **new** and wild
      delight.

Ere **the sun had** drunk his **dew-wine from the** chalice
      of the morn,
I had gone to fetch her favour from the nooklet in the
      thorn,
Where in a tiny hollow that some little bird had made,
I found a dainty posy left half hidden in the shade :

* Church Road, Harborne.

A slip of milk-white heather and a red geranium bloom,
A pansy and verbena of delicate perfume,
With a spray of tender maidenhair and sprig of crimson
  phlox,
Made the sweet-scented love letter dropped in that way-
  side box.

As I read each mystic syllable that morning o'er and
  o'er,
My love deciphered all it said, and asked for nothing
  more ;
And the sweet hieroglyphs I'll keep unto my latest day,
For fonder things they speak to me than written words
  can say.

There is no need for me to dwell on what sweet Lettie
  thought
About the heartless lad whom she had made almost
  distraught;
The lover o'er at Merriden her brother was I found ;
And we have lived next door to him since we were
  bridal-bound.

A MEMORY OF WILDERSMOUTH.

1837.

No black eye ever wore a brighter smile,
  Its radiant beauty glorified the face,—
And made one pause and wonder for awhile,
  As with its lustre it illum'd the place.
Oft have I, journeying over life's long mile,
  . Seen many a fairy form of maiden-grace,
Whose dimpled cheek and captivating wile
  Beam'd forth beneath a fall of dainty lace ;—
But, never one did so my soul beguile,
  As she who met me where the Wilder meets
The wild Atlantic surge, that rolls and beats
  Against the rocky ramparts of the Isle ;
And when I think of the entrancing one,
  I pity him no woman smiles upon.

TO CARRINA.

A SINGER in my Western ways
I sauntered carolling my lays.
A solo from the golden bill
Of blackbird, or a meadow-rill
Singing along some sunny dell
Would charm me like a wedding bell.

Anon a wildling in the moss,
Or cowslip, or the Whitsun-boss ;
Or butter-blob, or lady smock,
Or willow, fern, or lichen'd rock
Did make me halt and pencil down
The thoughts that danc'd beneath my crown.
And when the throstle tun'd his throat,
Or lark into the blue would float,
Or dropping from the clouds above
Dart like an arrow to his love,
I sought in a sweet, simple song
The passing pleasure to prolong.
Then lovers met me here and there
And begg'd the favour of an air ;
And Sorrow in her sable weeds ;
And Pity, with her kindly deeds,
Would ask a stave ; thus line by line
I learnt to like this task of mine :
And since you bribe me with a smile
To pen a pleasant word or two,
May love and joy your way beguile
And health your rosy youth renew.

Harborne, June 9th, 1877.

ON THE FELLING OF FRANKLEY BEECH.

Alas ! thou'rt gone ; the axe has laid thee low ;
  The pride of all the landscape is no more ;
We called thee ours because we loved thee so,
  And sooth the loss has left us very poor.
By whose proud mandate was the dire act done ?
  What sacrilegious hand performed the deed ?
Who dared in presence of the glorious sun
  To smite and wound, and make thy old heart bleed ?
Thou had'st possession of the pleasant height,
  And stood in glory on its sunny crown,
And held it by an undisputed right,
  And yet some wanton hand must strike thee down.
Methinks I feel the force of every blow,
  And my soul quivers with the deadly stroke,
That sent thee thundering to the ground below,
  With a loud crash that boughs and branches broke.
They might have spared thee for the poor man's sake,
  Whose pleasures are but few amid his toil,
And wrought their mischief in some neighbouring brake,
  Where furze and brushwood never fail the soil.
How thou didst gladden the wayfarer's heart !
  What pleasure thou didst yield the poet's eye !
How oft the painter, faithful to his part,
  Hath wedded thee to his bright summer-sky.

The lambs were happier **when** thou wert there ;
   And larks sang merrier upon the wing ;
The herds more cheerful looked, the flocks more fair,
   And sweeter scented were the flowers of Spring.
The townsman, standing on the fair browed hill
   Of windy Harborne, looking to the West,
Of the broad sweeping view would take his fill
   From Clent to Norton ; then midway, at rest,
His gaze would dwell on **thy** commanding form
   Central, **and** sovereign **of the vast** expanse,—
Oft thinking how defiant of **the storm**
   Thou held'st thy own in **the tumultuous dance.**
But now he turns with **an averted eye,**
   Since ruthless hands have **marred** the **lovely scene,**
And hurrying past, for love's sake heaves **a sigh,**
   And grieves a vandal's **axe** could **be so keen.**

LOVE IN SUNSHINE.
SONG.

When Memory, like **fairy May,**
   Repairs unto her **fragrant bower,**
Where Love sat every **sunny day**
   In dalliance with his darling **flower ;**
And fancy paints each bygone scene
   In fresh and glowing colours dight,
And like the young moon smiles serene
   On her creation of delight ;—

Our weary life renews her youth,
   And treads once more the olden ways,
While rosy Innocence and Truth
   Sing o'er their long forgotten lays—
Until the heart enchanted beats
   With strong pulsating thrills of joy,
And Earth grows rich in vernal sweets,
   And Rapture dances like a boy.

Then Memory weave thy magic spell,
   Recalling all those golden **dreams**
Of bliss which we **were** wont to tell
   Beside the softly singing streams ;
When every dewdrop **was a gem,**
   And every star an angel's eye ;
Since love was life's bright diadem,
   And Sorrow had no time **to sigh.**

THE LOVE LETTER.

SONG.

SUNG BY MADAME **RUDERSDORFF.**

ANOTHER letter ! and from him !
   With Cupid on the cover.
'T will be a very harmless whim,
   I'll fancy him my lover.

He calls me jewel, pretty pet,
  And sends his love to mother,
And vows he never shall forget
  My face for any other.
"'Tis very hard," he writes, "for me
  To play a part so shy.
Why keep me in suspense?" says he,
  I cannot tell him why.

My mother told me yesternight,
  That ten was out of season;
And ask'd why Rob kept out of sight,
  She said she had her reason,
I stammer'd out a something, when
  She stopped me : " No inventions;
Beware of those deceitful men.
  Pray, what are his intentions?"
I would have told her all I knew;
  When, lo ! a heavy sigh;
And such a simpleton I grew;
  I cannot tell you why.

But Robin's letter, thus he writes :
  " Sweet Jessie, one word—never
Shall I forget that night o' nights
  I thought thee mine for ever"
Poor Robin ! but I'll read no more;
  There's some one hither rushing.

That's mother's footstep on the floor;
 I fear she'll catch me blushing.
" What, Jessie ! what are you about ?
 A love-letter ! O, fie !"
I couldn't blurt the secret out,
 And cannot tell you why.

It's no use going on like this ;
 To *lose* him there's the danger.
'Tis heaven ordains a woman's bliss
 Should settle on a stranger.
If love makes hearts go pit-a-pat,
 My own has just that feeling ;
And so I'll write him tit for tat,
 Without a thought concealing.
" Dear Rob, in answer to your prayer,
 I send you this reply :
Yes ! thine for ever, Jessie Clare !"
 Girls better love than die.

THE REQUEST.

When I am gone one thing I ask of thee,
 I know thou wilt vouchsafe to grant the boon,
Take up thy pen and write my elegy,
 A sweet love-lyric to a happy tune.

You know I gave my all, my love, my life,
    To paint Devonia's solitary nooks,
And moorland-floods white-lipp'd with foam and strife,
    Her storm-swept tors and softly murmuring brooks.
Say then, that Nature claimed me for her own ;
    That Beauty won my heart while yet a child,
And dear to me was every moss-clad stone,
    Each reed-thatched cottage, lane and floweret wild.
How naiads watched me from each rocky stream,
    And dryads from each deep umbrageous wood,
Till life became a soft delicious dream,
    And poesy as sweet as angel's food.
Say, too, like Joshua in days of yore
    I bade the sun at my command stand still,
And charmed the mad waves breaking on the shore,
    And saved the ruin on the castled hill.
For love of Art I ask it more than fame,
    And love of thee whose love can not deny ;
To thine own pastoral music set my name,
    And I will lay me down in peace and die.

THE ELEGY.*

I PROMISED him that I would not **forget**,
 To carry out **his** last and fond request ;
And since to Nature he has paid his debt,
 Peace to his ashes !—let the good **man rest.**
The gentlest, meekest son of Earth was he,
 Beloved and loving—simple as a child,
Yet deeply learned in Art's sweet mystery,
 He revelled in the beautiful and wild,—
The broad champaign, the cattle-dotted meads,
 Idyllic scenes where living waters flow,
Gold iris, **bulrush, and** green marish reeds,
 Rich crimson sunset and soft afterglow ;
And hamlets on the margin of my † Exe ;
 The patient teams while busy at **their toil ;**
The rosy beauty of the gentler sex ;
 And honest ploughman ruddy as the soil.
And as the master of the tuneful Art,
 Harmoniously **the** various chords will blend,
Till each of each becomes a magic part
 And one rich concord the triumphant end,—

---

* OBITUARY NOTICE.—At his residence, Parker's Well
Cottage, Topsham Road, near Exeter, Mr. William Traies,
Artist, aged 83.—*Western Times,* **April 28,** 1872.

† The author **was born on** "The Ham," **by the Exe,**
Tiverton, North **Devon, Jan.** 21st, **1819.**

So **layer upon** layer deftly laid,
  Of glowing colour from his subtle **brush,**
Gave us a cloudless June-sky, golden-ray'd,
  Over the green haunts **of** the merry thrush.
And all so mellow'd that we felt the charm
  For ever present **in** his dreamy glades;
That light which steeped in bliss the homely farm,
  And the translucent darkness **of his** shades.
His **inspiration** from the bright he drew,
  His cheerfulness made **him** an inward heaven,
And gave his landscape that celestial hue,
  Which proves the painter's Paradise is Devon.

THE HONEST MAN.

SONG.

A song, **a** lusty-hearted song !
  Come join me as I sing,
Though Might be Right and Right be Wrong,
  Still Honesty is king ;
The sovereign of a monarchy,
  Built on the good old plan,
That to be strong we must be **free,**
  And **every** one a man,
          All-round,
          Heart-sound,
      Base manœuvres scorning ;

Upright
And down-straight,
Like six o'clock **i'** th' morning.

The offspring of an erring race
    Some blemish you may find,
But with a joy-illumin'd **face**
    And pity for his kind ;
With soul to succour the distress'd,
    And charity to scan
The failings of the worst and best
    Each one should play the **man ;**
        All-round,
        Heart-sound,
    Base manœuvres scorning,
        Upright,
    And down-straight,
Like six o'clock i' th' morning.

True, one **may** lack the golden store
    Which Avarice will hoard,
But none must dare to call him **poor**
    Whom Nature makes **a lord ;**
Who from his little gives his mite
    Gaunt misery to ban,
And boldly **stands up for the right**
    A brave **and dauntless** man,

All round,
Heart-sound,
Base manœuvres scorning,
Upright,
And down-straight,
Like six o'clock **i' th'** morning.

Such men at times we may behold,
  Majestic in **their** mien,
Who, two-and-twenty-**carat gold**,
  Of sterling worth **are seen** ;
While some we loved are now at **rest**,
  Cold, cheerless, **mute** and **wan**,
Where Truth has **written on their breast**,
  " He lived and died a man,
All-round,
Heart-sound,
Base manœuvres scorning,
Upright,
And down-straight,
Like six **o'clock i' th'** morning."

And **when we** shall be carried **hence**,
  To moulder in the dust,
Be this our labours' recompense,
  The honour of the just.

Some sorrow-pearls we too would crave,
 Shed only as love can,
And **this to mark** our humble grave,
 " Here lies an honest man.
  All-round,
  Heart-sound,
Base **manœuvres** scorning,
  Upright
  And down-straight,
Like six o'clock i' th' morning."

HURRAH FOR THE SUNSHINE.

SONG.

HURRAH for the sunshine ! Good-bye **to the** rain !
'Tis Summer, soft sunny, bright Summer again ;
The meadow's brown seraph sings high in the cloud,
And the scythes of the mowers are ringing aloud,
Hurrah for the sunshine ! **Good-bye to** the rain !
The corncrake is here with the cuckoo again.

Hurrah **for the sunshine** ! the glory of earth,
And smile of delight she puts on in her mirth,
The joy of the young, and the life of the old,
As they bathe in the meadowlands flooded with gold,
Where kingcups, enchanted, are watching again
God's far-away flocks on His indigo plain.

Hurrah for the sunshine ! Good-bye to the blight,
The blast-blow by day, and the mildew by night,
For the warm wind is here from the sea in the south,
With the scent of a cinnamon-spray in its mouth.
Hurrah for the sunshine ! Good-bye to the rain !
The swift screams aloud in its hawking again.

Hurrah for the sunshine ! Good-bye to the gray,
The badge of the March and the bane of the May,
For the queen of the seasons is out with her bees,
Where the odorous heather-hills sweeten the breeze ;
Hurrah for the sunshine ! Good-bye to the rain !
The swallows are high in the welkin again.

Hurrah for the sunshine ! Good-bye to the gloom :
An angel of light into Misery's room,
It steals by a way that no honey-bine knows
Entwined with the jessamine, ivy, and rose ;
Then fair fall the sunshine !—and speed to the rain—
Sweet sunshine, the charmer and solace of pain.

Hurrah for the sunshine ! Good-bye to the hail,
The race of the rack, and the surge of the gale,
For the tempests that gathered their hosts in the sky
No longer in fury go storming on high ;
'Tis calm in the heavens, and tranquil below,
Where balmy hedge-hawthorns are white with their
     snow.

Hurrah for the sunshine ! **Hurrah** for the lanes !
Where fragrant geraniums burn red through the panes,
And bonny green climbers that trail o'er the doors,
Paint fairy-like forms on the cottagers' floors.
Hurrah for the sunshine ! Good-bye to the rain !
The dog-roses nod to the poppies again.

Hurrah for the sunshine ! Good-bye to **old care** !
The **blue bell of** Heaven is blooming and fair,
And friendly boughs wave their broad **fans in the
    glade**
Where wayfarers **rest in the cool of the shade.**
Hurrah for the sunshine ! **Good-bye** to **the rain** :
The elder is creamy **with blossom** again.

" **Hurrah** for the sunshine !" the little ones shout,
As Age, on his crutches, once more hobbles out,
Where birds blithely warble, and love-couples greet
The butterflies, spinning around at their feet.
Hurrah for the sunshine ! Good-bye to the rain !
The merry haymakers are busy again.

Hurrah **for** the sunshine ! **The folk are away**
To the kingfishers' haunt, **where the** blue-dragons play,
And cattle knee-deep in **the willowy brooks**
Make pictures for painters in fern-feathered nooks,
While midges, **that** sport in **the heart** of the glen,
Dance fairy quadrilles **for the poet again.**

Hurrah for the sunshine ! Good-bye to our fears !
God's will aye be welcome—but corn in **the ears,**
And a green aftermath, **and a** stack of sweet hay,
With a pledge of rich fruitage, give life to a lay.
So hail to the sunshine ! Good-bye to the rain !
'Tis Summer, **old** sunny, bright Summer again !

TO THE ADIANTUM.

GATHERED AT THE TORS, ILFRACOMBE ; AND PRE-
SENTED TO THE AUTHOR, BY MISS B——. OCT. 1878.

I SEE thee, and am holden with a spell,—
    A willing slave of an enchanting dream.
The air is tuned, as if a silver bell
    Had caught the sweet wild music of a stream.
That trickling down some warm secluded dell,
    Bright flashing in the golden summer beam,
    Goes softly singing evermore—" Farewell,"
Where the blue lightnings of the dragons gleam.
    Thou darling of the fairy-fronded race,
I deemed the lady-fern was more than fair,
    But thou excelleth her in charm and grace,
And bear'st thyself with such a witching air
    That I some truth in the old fable see,
Save that Narcissus would have worshipped *thee*.

TO J. T. T----

A POSY FOR THE BRIDAL.

Good morrow, friend, long tried and true,
As fresh as April's early dew.
To see thee is the cure of care—
And looking on thy visage, fair
And smiling as a summer's morn,
I dream of valleys bright with corn
And pleasant woods and sunny glades,
And winding lanes with cooling shades
Away beside the Severn sea
Where long ago I met with thee.
And yet thy locks of silver gray
Show me that Time has been at play
With wanton fingers here and there ;
Thy brow, too, bears the marks of care
And sorrow for the dear ones gone,
Who sleep beneath the graveyard stone :
But health still revels on thy cheek,
And, full of fire, I hear thee speak,
And see the old flash in thine eye
And form that steps in triumph by.
I wept with thee in days of woe,
And when thy cup would overflow
With joy, I sang my sweetest strain
To make it overflow again.

And now I pipe a merry lay
To add a pleasure to the day *
When worthy Tucker's scion found
The sweetest flower of Osborne's ground.
O happy man ! did he but know
The worth which words must fail to show
Of her who now will bear his name,
His heart would burn a living flame,
So loving is she, and so kind—
With all adornments of the mind.
We knew her mother, know her sire—
The first we loved, the last admire.
So gentle was the Mother, she
Who weds thy son must gentle be ;
So good the Father that her name
Is fair already with his fame. †
And now God bless thy family,
All those that are, and those to be,
And, as all fragrant was the time
With honeysuckle-scented lime,
When Leslie to the altar led
His Florence with her timid tread,

---

* August 9th.

† Alderman Osborne, J. P., is a gentleman much esteemed in the Midlands for his works' sake, and, as the originator of the Birmingham Free Library, he has been honoured with the public Presentation of his Portrait, which now hangs in the Art Gallery of that town.

So may their future sweetened **be**
With health, love, joy, and amity;
And parents long survive to share
The blessings of the Happy Pair.

Harborne, Aug. 13th, 1877.

TO THE LATE SIR **THOMAS** DYKE ACLAND, BART.

ON HIS EIGHTIETH BIRTHDAY.

FORCED by the potent laws of love and **duty**
  To leave the fragrant valleys of the **west**;
A **sigh** for home and old Devonia's beauty,
  Is the **chief** tenant of **my** yearning **breast**.

What boots it that the meadows here are yellow,
  With spotted cowslips ruffled to the rim,
Or that the lark salutes his happy fellow
  O'er azure harebells dewy to the brim?

What **though the sun** should gild **the** morn **with**
      splendour,
  And the white moon walk **in** her light **on** high,
And night, rich with the glory planets **lend** her,
  Scatter her **starry** treasures **o'er the sky**?

To me, with **my** poor vision disenchanted,
  Night is a vault which sepulchres the day;
The moon is but a ghost in chamber haunted,
  The sun is blind, and darkness is his ray?

O for Devonia's daffodils that ever
  Burst into bloom and beauty like a flame !
And primroses which fringe each wood-crowned river,
  And speedwells, with their sweet poetic name !

With these the rose herself, the red and royal,
  In some far shade may hide her head and blush ;
And though I may be counted most disloyal,
  Ten nightingales for *one* Devonian thrush.

But whither is my wayward fancy straying ;
  Thou dear Devonia art my golden dream ;
And thus my pen has been the vagrant playing,
  When Acland's virtue should have been the theme.

Forgive my fault, if in my warm affection
  My thought took wing at the reveréd name,
And speeding then in quest of fair perfection,
  Dreamt Acland and Devonia were the same.

Thou wilt not blame the minstrel, if in singing
  A love-lay for his county he should blend
The deeds of him who praised his first rhymes' ringing,
  And sank the patron in the generous friend.

Beloved by all, the lowly and the mighty,
  Thy name, Sir Thomas, is a pleasant sound,
Which grows more dear at the ripe age of eighty
  To all the dwellers in the country round.

And looking on thee, what is their ambition ?
  To be what thou art, noble, loving, kind ;
Great pattern men, and this is their petition,
  " O may we leave as good a name behind."

Behind—alas ! yes e'en the best must perish,
  All that is mortal must return to dust ;
But actions die not ; these thy friends will cherish,
  And write upon thy tomb, " Here lies the just."

Rock Cottage, Harborne, Birmingham, April, **1867.**

" APRIL FOOLING."

" I CANNOT tell the reason why
  The first of April we decry
    And call it All Fools' day ;
It seems to me to be a crime,
For then the Spring is in its prime
    And brighter oft than May.

'Tis very true I will agree,
No matter what the season be,
    We've fools enough, alack !
And those the biggest idiots are
And under an unlucky star
    Who've Mischief at their back.

This was old Ruth's soliloquy
That morning o'er her toast and **tea,**
And Ruth was counted wise;
And that she was so you will find
If you will only be so kind
To read with open eyes.

'Twas on the thirty-first of March
When maiden buds upon the **larch**
Were greening **by the brake,—**
That Ruth o'erheard a neighbour say
A word which made **her haste away**
Her thirsty **ire to** slake.

A half o' hint that so and so
Had said an evil thing or two
Against the worthy dame;
Insinuating this, in fact,
That she had done some foolish act
Which tarnished much her fame.

And so she made this solemn vow,
" I ere the sun on Walton **Brow**
To morrow morn shall rise,
Will go and ask the wicked **lout**
What he has had to say **about**
Myself, **to** his surprise."

The morning came, and forth she went,
Where violets were sweet with **scent**,
   And snowdrops all in bloom,
And many a golden crocus cup
Was smiling that the lark was up
   In Heaven's own ante-room.

And then the thrush began to **sing**
To his blithe brother on **the wing**,
   And now the mellow merle,
Until the tomtit at his play
Made merry as a popinjay
   With Poll the milking girl.

"**O** what a joyous time" said Ruth,
"**The** Universe is in its youth
   And full of love and joy ;
How sad it is to think that men
Will work their fellows bitter pain,
   And so their peace destroy.

But I must hie me to the loon
Who told his folly to the moon
   When speaking light of me ;
And such a lesson he shall learn
That he henceforward will discern
   'Tis better mute to be."

With that her hands clutched at the air,
Then said with **mirth** provoking stare,
 " Lor what a dunce to school ;
I see old Peter was at play
At **Maygames** long before the May,
 I'll be no April **Fool.**"

So all good folk take **my advice,**
Before you act consider **thrice**
 About the things **you** hear ;
And of half-hinters **have a care,**
They're Mischief's **imps, so pray** beware,
 And you'll have **less to fear.**

April 1st, 1879.

———

TO D. D———

ON HIS PRESENTING THE **AUTHOR WITH A POSY** OF ROSES.

THOUGH words are poor, **when** feeling moves
The **soul** to paint the thing **it loves,**
Yet **know** a happy man is **he**
Who links himself in sympathy
With everything of beauty borne
At **noon, at eve,** at night, or morn :—

N

But he whose dear delight, is this,
To woo young Summer's maiden kiss
Among his rosebuds, happier lives
When he from his abundance gives,
And, in bestowing, doth believe
'Tis better far than to receive.

POETICAL PERCEPTION.

THE daisy hath an influence
Which asks of man another sense,
Ere he can apprehend the power
In the pure nature of the flower.

LOVE IN ENGLAND.

"ONE TOUCH OF NATURE MAKES THE WHOLE
WORLD KIN."

A MEMORY of a happy day.—
    My friend as we were strolling out,
Turned up a little narrow way,
    Not heeding what he was about.

A pleasant, deep, and winding lane,
   Cutting the skirts of down and dell,
With peeps of castle, cot, and fane,
   Mill, river, bridge, and mossy well.

Green ivy-nooks alive with fern,
   And flowers that made the wayside fair
Confronting us at every turn,
   Fast held the soul as with a snare ;

Here Nature's little saintly nun,
   The wee white daffodil would gleam ;
There celandines, that love the sun,
   Ran down the bank a golden stream,

While all the woods sweet music made,
   For linnets, led off by the thrush,
A concert held in every glade,
   Nor ceas'd until the twilight hush.

" O what a song of wild delight
   Those birds are trilling, prithee hark !"
Broke out my friend, as to his sight
   Mine eyes shone with a joyous spark.

But I had caught another sound,
   Which made my heart with rapture dance ;
And as along the lane I wound
   I yearn'd to catch a wish'd-for glance.

You guess the signal that I heard ;
　My friend, he wot not of **the** sign,
She came, his soul was wildly stirr'd ;
　"Too late," I said, "for she is mine."

LOVE IN INDIA.

(FROM HAFIZ.)

WHERE Sindhu's waters flash and glide,
　Her eye the orient sun did shame ;
Of Hindustan she was the pride,
　I ask'd the favour of her name ;
When, toying with a raven curl,
　The Maiden answer'd " Lily."—Pearl—
" For me, for me, Sweet ?" " Lula."—No—
　Ah ! that she should have answer'd so !

ABILITY AND CONCEIT.

THE throstle waits **with** folded wing
　His richest melody to sing,
While the pert sparrow will essay
　A chirp or twitter every day.

TO A. B. P——

As erst the clouds flew ramping past,
    Like sleuth hounds o'er the earth,
Fierce-eyed and furious on the blast,
    To chase the hours of mirth,
I sought thy cosy ingleside,
    Where peace and comfort smile,
In converse sweet at eventide,
    A moment to beguile.

And pleasant 'twas to read with thee,
    Our grand old bard sublime,
Who sung that mighty mystery,
    Before the birth of time—
How Paradise, the fair, was lost,
    And how it was regained.
When Satan and his vanquished host,
    For evermore were chained.

Or as the daylight would depart,
    Beneath the summer sky,
To watch Diana shoot her dart,
    With diamond barb on high,
Or mark old Cader in the cloud;
    That hung above our head,
As plain as when from mist and crowd,
    We trod the Mawdach's bed,

Delightful are the quiet hours,
  That I enjoy with thee,
At sundown mid the birds and flowers,
  With thought and fancy free.
And long as life with thee shalt last,
  May Peace and Pleasure come,
To make as in the happy past,
  A halo for thy home.

Harborne, Christmas, 1879.

LOVE AT FIRST SIGHT.

He caught the sparkle of her bright blue eye,
  As one might, walking on the common way,
Catch a bright sun-gleam in the summer sky,
  And found it haunting him, both night and day.
He had gone out that morning in the May
  Unweeting who might be the passer by ;
But wherefore did he through the greenwood stray
  And be so wounded by a stranger ? why ?
Yet though but smitten by an artless maid,
  With just a rose and lily tinted cheek
And lip, where Love his little bow had laid
  Leaving behind a soft vermilion streak,
To heal the hurt in his sore heart and head,
  Th' unwary damsel he was fain to seek.

LOVE'S REBUFF.

What ails the fellow ? He is crazed, I trow,
  To talk unto a stranger in this way ;
  Woo me, indeed ! He's madman in the play,
And that I very soon to him will show.
He tells me he will never have my " No :"
  Well, be it so, then he must take my " Nay."
  I loathe him, and will keep the dog at bay
Until the fever of his heart is low.
  There's something wrong about this thing called love.
A silly frenzy made of sighs and gladness.
  A dual of contraries, fire and snow.
  He says he's found life's crown in me, Heigho !
If so, the gods must settle it above,
  Enamoured thus of Hate is arrant madness.

TO E. H. BURRINGTON ON THE DEATH OF HIS BROTHER FREDERICK.

Dear Friend of many years, in spirit true ;
For love of the old bygone, Peace to you.
It grieved me sore as I these tidings read,
" The Bard of Exon resteth with the dead."
Oft there are ties more dear than those of blood—
The bonds that wed the generous and the good,
And golden cords of poesy that bind
The heart with heart, and kindred mind with mind.

How blest the lot where *both* together meet,
The birth-link'd Brother and the Minstrel sweet.
Such was the joy which Heaven vouchsafed to you,
The double bond which love kept ever true.
As one may hear, when vernal eves are still,
A throstle singing on a neighbouring hill,
And, listening, catch a far-off answering strain,
Sent by a brother warbler o'er the plain :—
So have we heard your interchanging song,
A love-duet, float all the vale along,
As one more vigorous led the tuneful way,
And one with his sweet minor closed the lay.
Alas ! the loss.   See poor Devonia now
With Sorrow's cypress wreathes her lovely brow ;
For the sweet pipe of Larkbeare sounds no more—
While he, who sang the " Fishers " by her shore,
And Bydown's bard, whose heart-reviving song
Our soul's delight did evermore prolong,
Each with his silent harp upon a tome,
Sleeps with our brother in their last long home.
And yet the Muse of Isca should not weep
As if her cup of woe were overdeep,
Since you, who sang the " Beautiful " of yore,
And struck your lyre to animate the poor,
Shall take it once again and sweep the strings,
Till all the land with its sweet music rings.

Harborne, October 22nd, 1877.

THE BLIND BOY'S CAROL.

THEY are gone to gather holly,
  With its berries, red and bright,
Where the meadow-brook is frozen,
  And the meadow-land is white ;
And the children of the village
  Are with them full of glee,
Save the blind boy, who is absent
  In a Christmas reverie.

At the game of " Spin the Trencher,"
  He was quickest at the call ;
And in " Blindman's Buff," at catching,
  He was master of them all ;
While, in a fog, at " Stag Hunt,"
  He was foremost in the play,
Since ever, in the darkness,
  He was sure to find his way.

Now, in a cosy corner
  Of his cottage, by the fire,
With his face turn'd to the heavens,
  He is sitting with his lyre ;
And, when his song he singeth,
  No neighbours dare intrude,
With gossip, o'er the threshold
  Of his happy solitude ;—

For he looketh then **so** radiant
  With his little sightless eyes,
That he seems to be, in spirit,
  Away in Paradise—
And wandering with the seraphs,
  Where God's own lilies grow
Beside the sea of jasper,
  In raiment white as snow.

But, the **sweetest of his carols**
  He chaunteth at the **time**
When the shepherds heard the angels,
  A most delicious rhyme
Of wild Judean mountains,
  And rivers of the plain,
As if the winds and waters
  Were warbling in his strain.

And then, he sings of Joseph,
  And Mary, and her joy,
When first she saw her infant—
  The little Hebrew boy ;
And of a holy vision,
  The blind can only see,
Like good old Bartimeus
  Of blessed memory.

O for the light and glory
  On that little blind boy's face,
As he sings **with soul** enraptured
  His lay of love and grace !
For, like the sons of Beulah,
  His countenance doth shine
With the beauty of an angel,
  Celestial, and Divine.

Christmas, 1880.

" YOU'D NOT SERVE DANDA SO."

Two fiddlers met in merry June,
  Their friendly bows **to try ;**
The fiddle **of** one **was** well in tune,
  The other a note too high.
" T'sha," hiss'd out **he that led the way,**
  " That is too bad, you know ; "
The other had not **a word to** say.
  " You'd not serve **Danda so.**"

" **Come,** give your string another screw,
  And try the chords again."
Both, without any more ado,
  Commenced the former strain.

"There, now you're galloping too fast.
        Why don't you play more slow?"
And then, which made him stand aghast,
    "You'd not serve Danda so."

Who Danda was, or what it meant,
        The question is, you see,
Was it the man who wanted rent
        Of Mister Tweedledee?
Whoe'er he was, it matters not;
        But this I wish to show:
Old Tweedledum's was very hot.
    "You'd not serve Danda so."

Full many a moon has waned since then,
        And many a sun has set,
And many a band of fiddling men,
        I often must have met;
But whatsoever I am at,
        Or wheresoe'er I go,
This saying evermore comes pat,
    "You'd not serve Danda so."

All have their Danda in the round
        Of life, a friend, or pet;
And jealousy is always found
        Inclined to fume and fret;

And if, perchance, you' make a slip,
  Which we must often do,
You're sure to feel this cutting **whip**,
  " You'd not **serve Danda** so."

But there's one **thing we all should mind**,
  As we go on our way,
To learn the art of being **kind**,
  And prove it every day ;
And if we act the friendly part,
  As here and there we go,
No one will cry out, stung at **heart**,
  " **You'd** not serve Danda so."

THE HAPPY MERMAN.

ADDRESSED TO " CHARLIE CANDOUR."

A ROLLICKING **Johnny o' Dreams**,
  I am here in the **valley** at Score,
Where the woodlands **are** wooing the streams,
  Hence this ditty to **you,** *a la* Moore.

I would I could sing you the joy
  I have felt since I entered the town ;
You will say, " I believe you my boy,"
  And toss on my letter to Brown.

They may prate, as you write, of Torquay,
  Of Scarborough, Brighton, and Rhyl;
But a "coombe" in North Devon for **me**,
  With the mermaidens under the hill.

To be candid, dear Candour, the girls
  That I meet in the meadows by chance,
Are of all bonny maidens the pearls;
  And life is a happy romance.

Already **the pet of the** dames,
  Fan, Florry, **Loo,** Ada, and Nell,
Shy Patty, and Ruth are my flames,
  And Deborah, **Dolly, and** Bell.

I have Cicely, too, **and Celine,**
  Luce, **Tilly,** Maria, **and** Maud,
Eliza, and gay Josephine,
  Who always are talking of Claude.

Next Marion, Ella, and **Moll,**
  Sly Gwendoline, Dora, and Kate;
Rose, Thomasine, Rhoda, and Poll,
  And pretty Jemima **to mate.**

Then Eva, **the light of the lane,**
  With **bryony berries and ferns,**
Bewitches, **and dear Sarah Jane,**
  And I worship the bunch, *a la* Burns.

But, as the base " Varmint " of old
    Stole into the fairest of spots,
So here is Xantippe, the scold,
    The plague of poor Zebedee Potts.

That termagant Jezebel, too,
    Well known by the tilt of her nose ;
Don't care about taming a shrew,
    Nor you, Mister C., I suppose.

So sighing **for** quiet and rest,
    I wandered alone by **the sea,**
To à cave in this Gem of the West,
    Where a mermaid sat smiling at me.

Sat under the King of the Tors,
    As bright as a gull in the bay,
Or **snowdrops** when fresh from their " mors," *
    And **sweet as a lily** in May.

'Twas rapture **and love at first** sight ;
    And now by a myrtle **in bloom,**
With Ilfra to charm and **delight,**
    I am happy—

        THE MERMAN O' 'COOMBE.

Ilfracombe, October 2nd, 1878.

---

* Devonshire word for " **roots.** "

"THE SWAN OF ISCA." *

A LOVE-GIFT FROM EXON TO IONA.

" 'Tis a far cry to fair Loch Awe,"
But love o'errides the Highland saw—
For let an ocean freeze between
The land where human want is seen,
Or broad Saharas scorching lie
Beneath a burning Tropic sky,
In spite of what the heartless say,
Sweet Charity will find a way.

And such a sight my vision sees
Away in the wild Hebrides,
Where moving mountains of the deep,
Round Argyll's brightest jewel sweep;
Where seagull, cormorant, and shag,
And tern and puffin dot the crag,
With perigrine and guillemot,
That haunt the legendary spot.

There when the ragged rack-clouds frown,
And winter floods are pouring down,
And homeless winds, by tempest driven,
Fly shrieking through the vault of heaven;
The fisher folk their task must ply
Beneath the black-browed thunder sky,

---

* A Fisherman's boat.

And boldly daring, bravely ride
The storm-ridged levin-lighted tide.

With loyal heart and iron nerve,
From duty's path they scorn to swerve,
E'en though a sad prophetic boom
Fills every cabin full of doom ;
But when the hurricanes are slipp'd,
Like sleuth hounds, fierce and fiery-lipp'd,
And mad tornadoes lash the main,
Ah ! what avails their courage then ?

O ! Bourg, Ben More, and Loch-na-kael,
Could mutter many a fearsome tale
Of cries heard in the dark, and then
The coasts thick strewn with drownéd men ;
And Staffa's rock, with Fingal's cave,
Could tell how loud the whirlwinds rave,
And, with a fury's fell delight,
Chase down the fishers in their fright.

And Reileg Ordrhain's stones and turf,
Might speak of wreckage in the surf ;
And mothers' moans and widows' tears,
And maidens over lovers' biers ;
While St. Columba's cell could say
How holy fathers came to pray,
That He, who rules the sea, would keep
The souls upon the raging deep :

o

Then Jura wail his woeful song,
And Morven the sad strain prolong,
And Mull's high towering mountain, too,
The direful story might pursue ;
And stern Cape Wrath, of dreadful fame,
Tell the black legend of its name,
Till not a woman's cheek were dry,
Or man's keen-sighted eagle eye.

But mercy tempers every woe,
Thus, when the wildest tempests blow.
Our God gives in the hour of need
An opening for the kindly deed ;
And hence, in fair Devonia's land,
Is seen a friendly outstretched hand,
As Charity, with radiant smile,
Links Exon to the holy isle.

Our " Swan of Isca," we would make,
More dear than that on Mary's lake ;
An ark of refuge on the sea ;
A timely aid in penury ;
A messenger, by Pity sent,
On heaven's own work of mercy bent :
Love weds the twain, 'tis nobly done,
See Exon and Iona one.

FORSAKEN LOVE.

IF one has seen a broken rosebud swing
The helpless victim of each ruthless wind,
And watch'd it buffet with the storm unkind
That toss'd and vex'd it with its wanton wing;—
Or met a wounded dovelet on his way,
The pretty fondling of its parents' nest,
With pensive upturn'd eye and timorous breast,
And found it sadden some sweet afterlay:—
He will not look upon a wasted love
As sport for jesting, or a sight to flout,
But think 'twere better that life's light were out
Than one should bear this blessing from above,
God's crowning passion in the human heart,
As but an idle thing to die apart.

POETIC PLEASURES.

OF all the moments poets prize,
   None dearer are than those
In which their maiden-thoughts arise,
   As song unbidden flows ;—
Then sing they in their spirit-flight
   The lark-notes of their lay,
And welcome with a pure delight
   The soul's high holiday.

And I have known those happy times,
  Rich seasons of the mind,
When music with its fairy chimes
  Tuned every passing wind ;
Life's full flood-tides of ecstasy,
  When joy shone out a star,
The promise of felicity
  In brighter realms afar.

SONG OF THE EXMOOR HUNT.

THE CHASE OF THE WILD RED DEER.

**WRITTEN FOR THAT GRAND OLD VETERAN OF THE FIELD,
THE REV. JOHN RUSSELL.**

Hark ! hark to the horn ! how it rings in the ear,
Of the Exe and the Barle and the bonny red deer,
The harbourer's pride with his branches and tines,
A forest king bearing "his rights" for the "signs,"—
And Bissett afield on his stout trusty grey,
The Parson's black nag, and the Dulverton bay :
For the tufters are hard on their quest in the wood,
With snuffle and traverse and thirsting for blood,
When Challenger raises his head, giving tongue,
As the hazels go crash to the jolly old song,
" Hark back ! give him play, let him get well away,
Then off all together at 'Forrard !' Hooray !"

There's a northerly breeze blowing in from the sea,
  And the hunters are merry as merry can be,—
For the sun has popp'd out from his bed in the cloud
As the pack is laid on while bold Arthur, aloud,
Cries " Tighten your girths, they are hard on the spoor,
Its O for a jolly good run on the Moor."
Hark together ! Away ! we are off with a bound,
As the horn its tantivy, tantivy, doth sound,
For a warranted stag with his brow, bay, and tray,
Is making for Dunkery Beacon to-day.
" Hark together ! Away ! Hark together ! Away !
Hark ! Forrard together ! Hark ! Forrard ! Away ! !"

Just hear how they chirrup ! the running is hot,
No fear of a fault, they are right on the slot,
While Russell the lusty old Chief o' the Chase
Shouts " Swift as a brocket, too, look at his pace,
A six year old beauty, let's follow the spoor,
Its O for a jolly good run on the Moor !"
See ! see, how they swarm ! we are off with a bound,
And " Bird on the wing" runs as true as a hound,
As our right royal hart with his brow, bay, and tray
Makes straight for Black Barrow at Hark ! Hark
      Away !
" Hark together ! Away ! Hark together ! Away !
Hark ! Forrard together ! Hark ! Forrard ! Away ! !"

O'er hills, red with heather, combe, forest, and bluff,
We follow the line and the riding is rough,
For the " Cry " has been chiming its merriest tunes
From Dunkery hill to the vale o' the Doones;
So "Ware bog," the " Bay " makes amends for the
     toil,—
In Badgeworthy Water he's certain to soil,
Where Russell is **sure** in the pink o' the sport
To honour Jack Babbage when sounding the *mort*,—
And bearing off slot and broad antlers, hooray,
With "Now then my lads for the next Hark ! Away."
" Hark together ! Away ! Hark together ! Away !
Hark ! Forrard together ! Hark ! Forrard ! Away !!!"

THE STORM.

HARK to the pealing thunder-roll !
     While forks of living light
Destructive dart from pole to pole
     Athwart the wrathful night.

With terror flashing from her eyes,
     As loud the wild winds moan,
" God spare me for my babe !" outcries
     The Widow sad and lone.

Straight taken captive by his fear,
   Where flooding storm-clouds stream,
The Student turning lifts his ear,
   Oblivious of his theme.

Now filled with thoughts **of** dire remorse,
   The Wrecker in his den
Lives o'er his past misdeeds perforce,
   And thinks of drownéd men.

While little Innocents **abed**,
   Aroused from happy **dreams**,
Cling closer, being **sore afraid**,
   And watch for **morning-beams**.

O **Lord** ! most terrible art thou,
   How solemn is this hour !
The very heavens before Thee bow
   And own Thy mighty power.

A PORTRAIT.

I, **too**, would **be a** painter, **and will** try
   To paint my Daphne of this pleasant hill.
   Calm as a summer lake, when winds are still,
Beams her bright countenance, whose open eye,
And brow uplifted ever to the sky

Speak the observing power and master will,
Which bid her with rare hues her canvas fill
And woo dear Nature's secrets **with a sigh.**
But, mark her smiles, that do the lips **dispart !**
Those rosy guardians of Titania's pearls,
Love's pretty play-things, when he bribes the heart,
And stately mien ; and something **in her** curls,
A nameless negligence outstripping **art :**
Then tell me who's **my** paragon of girls.

MOUNTAIN LOVE.

THE mountains have **a** Sabbath of **their own,**
Their huge foundations are laid **deep in rest ;**
On their calm summits Peace has built **her throne,**
And Silence found **a** solitary nest.

Each mighty, snow-clad, everlasting **hill,**
A white-robed priest **in act** of worship stands :
With mute devotion all **the air is still,**
And Reverence gazes with uplifted hands.

The holy stillness reigning here is thine,
Fair maiden, perched upon those lofty crags,
And winds that, passing, chaunt their songs divine
To cloud-borne seraphs waving silver flags.

But what is it thou seest, mountain maid?
  Is it the shadow of some wandering kid?
Or **a** young mountaineer, who, half afraid,
  Hath from thy gaze a flitting moment **hid?**

It is so, **and** the home **of** the sublime
  Is dearer made by the **sweet** touch **of love;**
Love makes the beautiful **in every** clime,
  And adds a lustre to the **crowns above.**

That joy **be** ever with **thee, love's** pure **joy,**
  The **bliss** that reigned **in sinless** Paradise,
And kindles rapture **in** thy mountain-boy
  When welcomed **by the love-light** of thine eyes.

———

TWO SIDES TO A SAYING.

" NEVER swop horses when crossing **a stream.**"
Is right to a man who has sense **it** would seem ;
But suppose one has nought **but a** spavin'd old **mare,**
And the tide is too **strong** for **the** creature to bear,
And that right in the **middle she's** fast going down,
And the rider has **got an** objection to drown !
Why he's then a fool, or a middle-wit quite,
If **a better one's near,** not to snap at the bite.
Thus 'tis **oft with** old saws, as with very old friends ;
They're twisted, you see, to serve different ends.

DETRACTION

Seek not applause nor Fame's caress,
  If thou would'st tread a thornless way,
For 'tis the fate of all success,
  Detraction's penalty to pay.
To disappointed sloth and hate,
  E'en excellence becomes a crime,
And it is idle here to state,
  We know the reptiles by their slime.
Remembering, too, with certain men,
  'Tis easier to mar than make,—
Let incapacity complain,
  And from my rhyme this comfort take ;
The meanest cur that prowls the sod,
  Can soil the statue of a god.

THE JESSAMINE.

Just a glint o' morning sun,
  Just a blink o' summer-blue,
Had my pretty fragrant one,
  But the tale I'll tell to you.

In a dark and dingy lane,
  Hedged by walls of murky-brick,

Down below a cobwebb'd pane,
  Darkened o'er and dusted thick,
Grew a sickly jessamine,
  Grimy-green and sooty-white,
Which, whenc'er the sun got in,
  Strove to look a little bright.
How I watched the lovely thing !
  As it stretched towards the sky,
When its buds began to spring,
  And its flowers, too soon to die.
Once when bending o'er the wall,
  Listening to the sparrows' glee,
Lo, I spied a blossom small,
  Peeping o'er to look at me.
Happy in the transient gleam
  Of the sunshine, there it lay,
On the coping, like a dream,
  Smiling at the sunny day.
And I thought some fairy hand,
  Knowing how I loved the flower,
Had with its enchanting wand
  Made it bloom there for an hour.
Oh the worship in mine eyes !
  Oh the rapture in my heart !
And a loving sacrifice
  Soon was paid it on my part ;

But, alas, a wanton clutch
    Crushed my darling, fair and frail,
Did I prize my joy too much?
    I have told my simple tale.

TO LUCELIA.

WHEN beauty charms us with her smiles,
    Hard is the heart that will not bend ;
Fair woman all our woe beguiles,
    And I will be her constant friend ;
So lady take this pledge of mine,
    A token of the homage due,
From one who worships at the shrine,
    Where all the virtues welcome you.

YOUNG ASTRONOMERS.

THE moon was absent from the sky,
    Nor did the stars appear,
When Archie, lifting up his eye,
    " How dark 'tis Elfie dear !
I cannot see a star not one,"
    " Nor pritty mooney, brodder,"
" I wonder where they all are gone ?"
    " Dey gone to find der modder."

Harborne, January 23rd, 1880.

TO KATIE.

If it were mine the future to command,
   I'd have no briny tears thy bright eyes filling,
No sorrow-cloud should darken o'er the land ;
   And no disaster thy heart's bloom be killing.

Thy home should be a garden of delights,
   Thy walk a sunny path among the daisies ;
Thy haunts, the pleasant vales and wooded heights
   Melodious with the larks' and throstles' praises.

Thy skies should glisten with celestial forms,
   Like angels through ethereal regions flying ;
And Hope paint rainbows on the passing storms,
   And Music sing as down the sun sank dying.

Still if the Poet is a Prophet too,
   With clear prevision things to come foretelling,
And like thee, both to Art and Nature true,
   Then joy will be the inmate of thy dwelling.

Harborne. January 27th, 1879.

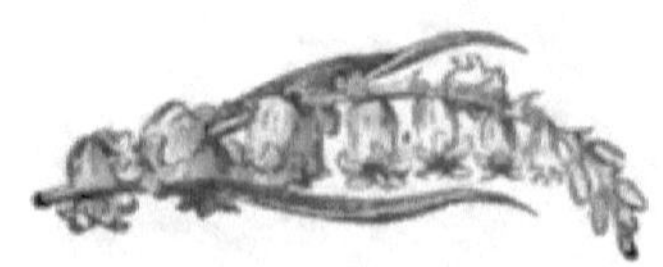

MORTHOE.

A WINDY moorland by the Western sea
Of evil omen, with a stone of doom,
On which, too oft, in the tempestuous gloom
Brave mariners, unweeting where they be,
Are dashed, alas, to perish hopelessly !
Yet even here the samphire shows its bloom,
And the wild thyme and heather, finding room,
Make a rich honey-harvest for the bee.
And, sweeter still, kind Hospitality,
Though rude in manners, plays her gentlest part
In welcoming the castaway ashore,—
Till all oblivious of his misery,
He blesses Heaven, and carries in his heart
The grand old form of SMITH for evermore.

Morthoe, October, 1878.

THE SNOWDROP.

HALTING in a lovely spot,
By a little mossy grot,
Where the summer shadows sleep,
And the zephyrs silence keep ;

Gazing on the herbage dun,
There I saw my floral nun,
All in dark-green raiment drest,
With her white **veil on** her breast.

Pensive, as a pious **saint,**
In the solemn **days of Lent,**
Motionless, she stood alone
Like **a statue cut in stone.**
Never mortal **so demure,**
Never virgin **half so pure,**
And a sanctifying **grace,**
Breathed around the holy place.

CARES.

WE must have cares !
The brightest cornfield **yieldeth** tares ;
And in our common atmosphere,
The sunniest time hath moving there
Vapours that float upon the air.
Thorns will o'erspread the flowering earth,
And roses give to canker birth ;
And soaring souls must be **deprest**
Ere they are perfected for rest.

A SKETCH FROM NATURE.

It was a dark and dreary day
   Which seemed a long and lingering dawn,
The earth was wrapped in misty gray,
Save when a little vagrant ray
   Flung a brief light o'er wood and lawn.

And drearier the picture grew,
   And heavier the leaden gloom,
When, as each hasty minute flew,
Death's signal-cord a sexton drew,
   And sent abroad the note of doom.

Yet lightly tripped the passers by,
   As if the world was full of joy,
Bright pleasure smiling in each eye ;
E'en Age jogged on without a sigh,
   As mirthful as a whistling boy.

Light as a fancy-pinioned thought,
   Our Ariel of the sky and cloud,
Leaving the nest his mate had wrought,
Went lilting up unharmed, though sought
   By slaves of the imbruted crowd.

Then throstles from **their** neighbouring **hills**
  Proclaimed **the near** approach **of Spring**
In loud and **interchanging trills,**
Mellifluent **as July rills**
  And **merry flutes when quavering.**

Thus life goes **ever, sun and shade,**
  The funeral bell, the jocund **song,**
The buds break, and **the blossoms** fade ;
Yet love has the arrangement made,
  That **Love which doeth** nothing wrong.

MY BROAD DOMAINS.

THE fair domains of Art are infinite !
  Beyond the golden shining of the sun,
Through realms supernal, yielding **new delight,**
  From **universe to** universe they **run.**
All is not **gathered** Beauty has **to give,**
  Still Proteus works with **his** transforming power,
Imagination doth **for ever live,**
  And there are charms unsung in every flower.
Thus feel I, as His **wide-resounding lay**
  I hear by th' **Almighty** master wrought ;
Then sauntering down some long-forgotten way
  Enriched by jewels which no eye has caught,
I hear strange melodies around me ringing
  Which long have waited for some poet's singing.

P

THE PASSING OF THE YEAR 1879.

I WATCHED alone to see the old year die,
  And saw the rack come racing up the West,
And, woe-bewildered, the pale stars on high
  Leap fitful through the rifts in their unrest.

When lo, would come low melancholy moans
  Of homeless winds, as sorrowful as knells,
With wandering night-birds' strange unearthly tones,
  And the harsh dissonance of jangled bells.

Then a wild tumult filled the sleeper's brain,
  Where the hoarse howlers with a horrid din,
Amid their orgies cried with might and main,
  " Ope wide the door and let the New Year in."

Thus was it then, and thus perchance 'twill be,
  As years, like kings, drop dying from their seat,
Some silent watcher will their passing see,
  While others revel on their winding sheet.

1879-1880.

JANUARY.

A REMONSTRANCE.

STERN Winter, with thy icy heart, avaunt !
Three moons of bitter frost should be thy share :—
Thou, like a miser, with penurious care
In heaping treasure, hast grown grim and gaunt.
Dost see the snowdrop in her ancient haunt
Pining for one sweet breath of southern air ?
And the mute skylark in his sleety lair,
Whose soul of courage not thy shafts can daunt ?
If still unmoved, have pity on the old
Who, starving by their fireless hearthstones, sit
Peering into the wild white waste of cold,—
While in the zenith, like a dead man's eye,
The sun, snow-blind, with spectral lamp unlit
Pleads, " Get thee gone, or let the famished die."

January 29th, 1879.

FEBRUARY.

How sweet it is to hail the opening year !
   And mark the budding of its early flowers,
As, in their season, all the tribes appear,
   To bless the moments of our leisure hours !

First comes the snowdrop with its saintly air,
   The mercury next, with blossoms dipped in green,
And now the hedgerows with white jacks are fair,
   While leafless coltsfoot gilds each sterile scene.

One law of beauty every plant illumes,
   For size and form we here examples see,
There richer tintings, and more odorous blooms,
   All true to station, order, and degree.

White, gold, and crimson, with an interchange
   Of violet, their several ends pursue ;
Charm linking charm in one long lovely range,
   From the nut's roselet to the lover's blue.

Harborne, February, 1879.

MARCH.

THE dark days are over, the Winter has gone,
   The voice of the turtle is heard in the land ;
The brooklet is singing that erst was a stone,
   And Spring, the Enchantress, is waving her wand.

The eyes that were dull, and the hearts that were sad,
   Are bright and aglow with the sunshine again ;
The little ones shout, and the linnets are glad,
   For the sleet and the blast are away o'er the main.

How cold was the earth, and how silent the sky,
 As the mountain lay stiff as a corse in its sheet:
And the sun in his icy pavilion on high,
 Glared out, like the dead, in a plague-stricken street.

What a change is abroad ! Hark ! our fellows in woe,
 The sparrows are chirping again on the eaves ;
And the throstle aloud in his prison below
 Is singing the love-song he learnt in the leaves.

Yes, Winter the stark and the dreary, has gone ;
 And, once more, the turtle is heard in the land.
The rivulet sings that was erst but a stone,
 For Spring, the Enchantress, is waving her wand.
1879.

APRIL.

How heavenly all ! the violets seem
 As if in Eden newly born ;
When Eve woke from her maiden dream
 Methinks 'twas such another morn.

The campion eyes the neighbouring sloe
 With amorous Spring's first flush of love,
Where wild pinks standing tip-o'-toe,
 Companion with the floral dove ;

While clouds bathe in the golden sheen
    Of brightest hours the day can make ;
And fond pairs, hedged in walls o' green,
    Find long lanes short for sweet love's sake.

Hark ! heard you not that merry shout ?
    A revel Nature holdeth there ;
In yonder wood young Life is out
    With all her children fresh and fair.

And list the distant village-tower !
    'Tis age grown garrulous with joy ;
As pattering like a silvery shower,
    Peals usher in a maiden coy—

First smiling here, then weeping there,
    To hide the sapphire in her eye,
An arch coquette, with jaunty air
    She wins each heart that passes by.

The cuckoo is her bird of song
    Since favourite of the year is she ;
And " Welcome, Welcome," all day long,
    " My pretty sweetling " singeth he.

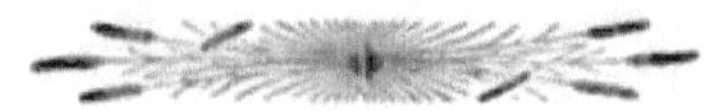

MAY.

May is here in frock of white ;
With her floral chrysolite ;
On the bank the primrose springs,
And with larks the welkin rings ;
See there, in the sunny lane !—
Bless her ! she is come again,
Hanging, on the spiky thorn,
Lamps to light the early morn.

Life, and Love, are on the hills ;
Cowslips wear their spotted frills ;
Meadow-maids their mottled studs ;
Daisies nod to yarrow buds ;
Campions with crimson flush ;
Violets begin to blush ;
Speedwell opens, too, her eye ;
And the king-cup woos the sky.

Here in dainty azure see,
As in merry mockery
Of the soft cerulean dome,
Blue-eyed hyacinth at home ;

Mark the herbage of the dells
Purpled with his faery bells—
Bells, which peal sweet notes of joy,
Heard by every truant boy.

Listen to the chattering pie,—
And the babbling jay's reply !
While the thrush repeats his song,
And the blackbird tunes his tongue.
Hear the chiff-chaff, finch and wren,
Gossiping in yonder glen,
Heedless of the cuckoo's lay,
" Woods all green, O ! come away."

Now all lovely things combine
To create a sense divine :
Young grass sweetens much the sight ;
Music gives the ear delight ;
Flowers make sweeter smell and touch ;
And of taste—say who o'ermuch
Beauty's honied lip can praise !
All those sweets bring sweet May-days.

JUNE.

WHO that has heard her loud and lusty lay,
  And lingering listened with his heart in tune,
And longs not for the maid that makes the hay,
  The blue-eyed beauty, rosy-bosom'd June ?

When soft delphiniums **rear on** lightsome **stalks**
  Their virgin tufts of hyacinthine flowers ;
And bright lupinas beautify our walks
  With their rich purples caught from rainbow-showers.

When o'er the arbour wave green willow wands,
  Throwing their shadows on dark culverkeys,
While neighbouring, high the bright laburnum stands,
  And swings its golden chains with every **breeze.**

And when the throstle soundeth **with** his horn
  His merry keynote for the matin strain,
As comes the gleam between **the** night and morn,
  Till one vast chorus rings o'er hill and plain,

How **sweet to** wander at the dawning hour,
  All lonely by a pleasant coppice-side !
Or **on** some crumbling battlemented tower
  To **hear** the feathered songsters in their pride.

Hark ! with a burst, the finches all **begin,**
　An ouzel, now, has joined the forest **quire,**
And **now** the blackcap, gushing like **a lyn,**
　Gives forth his lay, all melody and fire.

Anon the lark, saluting, hails the dawn,
　And from the meadow leaps into the cloud,
While from the umbrage of a neighbouring lawn,
　The cuckoo beats the time in bell-notes loud.

And O, to sit amid the thyme **and briar !**
　And list the runnel gurgling on its way !
And muse, as moved **by** reverent desire,
　The pious traveller halts awhile to **pray.**

And then to climb the steep and lofty hill,
　And **scent** the odour of the summer gale,
And looking **out o'er meadow,** moor, and **rill**
　Drink in the quiet of the peaceful vale.

And list the tinkle of the labour bell,
　And bellowing horn, made resonant by steam ;
Then homeward wend by some sequestered dell,
　And feast for ever on the lovely dream.

JULY.

Summer on the mountain,
  Summer on the plain ;
Summer, jocund summer,
  Cometh once again ;
With her eyes of sapphire,
  And her cheeks aglow,
Buxom as her sisters
  Ages long ago.

Summer in the woodland,
  Summer on the moor,
Peeping were the lilac
  Shades the cotter's door ;
Warbling in the welkin,
  Singing in the trees,
Breathing dainty odours
  On the gentle breeze.

Summer, when all bright things
  Merry-making meet,
When the meadow-meaders
  Make the valleys sweet ;
Summer, where the wind-rows
  Rustle in the sun ;
Summer, where the children,
  Blossom-laden, run.

Summer, with her fern-fronds
　　Feathering the lane ;
Lighting up the gold-cup,
　　Burnishing the vane ;
Tinting all the landscape
　　With her richest green ;
Making earth a palace
　　Worthy of a queen.

Summer in the garden,
　　Where the lily blows,
And the golden beetle
　　Nestles in the rose.
Summer, where the barkers
　　Strip their oaken wands ;
Summer by the sea-side,
　　Summer on the sands.

Summer in old England,
　　When in cowslip vales,
At the sound of " cuckoo,"
　　Lovers tell their tales.
Summer, when the church-bells
　　Ring their sweetest chime ;
Summer in my love's heart,—
　　Happy summer time !

AUGUST.

There's a mist o'er the meadow-land, mountain, and
    stream,
Young Morning has not yet awoke from her dream ;
Mute Poesy muses in peace by the mill,
And the trees are but shadowy clouds on the hill.

How rich the delight ! there's a charm in the time,
The honey's aroma is sweet in the lime ;
And a fairy like music, most welcome to me,
For a harper's abroad in the merry brown bee.

What a hush ! for a season, e'en labour is still,
And nothing is heard but the tink of a rill,
Or the sparrow's sharp chirp, as it strikes on the ear,
And the clarion challenge of bold chanticleer.

Alone I am monarch and lord of the sky !
The bird is my piper ; my hall is on high ;
And the landscape, that stretches away to the blue,
Is mine, by my birthright, with rapture to view.

In Barlow's Road, Harborne, 1878.

SEPTEMBER.

How sweet the waking of the Harvest morn !
   The sun's first look out o'er the eastern hill,
The smiles that sparkle on each dewy thorn,
   And soft September airs when clouds are still.

What bliss, then, seated on some upland stile,
   To hear the watchful scarecrow's " Hal-le-loo ! "
As his sharp sounding racket rings the while
   To fright away the little pilfering crew.

As up and up the bright sun rolls afar,
   Hill after hill comes peeping from the west ;
While, now and then, a church-vane, like a star,
   Gleams through the mist from some commanding
      crest.

How tranquil, too, the cattle look below,
   Reclining on their couches in the vale,
Or cropping the sweet herbage as they go
   With just a quiet flinking of the tail.

'Tis peaceful all, and if a sound is heard,
   It but intensifies the lovely charm ;
As when the shrill song of our gallant bird
   Breaks through the silence of an English farm.

Or when the starling's witching whistle steals
  Mellifluous upon the listening ear,
Or playing on his castanets, appeals
  For silence to some chirping robin near.

At such an hour the soul is wrapt in praise,
  As with a garment ; and amid the calm
Her song of thankfulness she, too, will raise,
  And fill the silence with a holy psalm.

The Hilly Fields, Harborne,
        September 6th, 1878.

OCTOBER.

IN MEMORY OF C. H. C.

THE wind is blowing winterley,
  The water-willow sighs,
And fitfully along the grove ;
  The yellow leafage flies.

The sun, as if in sympathy,
  Seems halting in the race,
As in the east the rounding moon,
  Half hides her pensive face.

Now trampling on the crumpled leaves,
  That spottles all the road,
Slow pacing to a new-made grave,
  Four neighbours bear a load.

While all around as solemnly,
  They near the final bourn ;
In plaintive accents tenderly,
  The bell is heard to mourn.

A gentle craftsman, like the bee,
  He lived among the flowers ;
So let him slumber peacefully,
  Among our pleasant bowers.

The desert blossomed like the rose,
  If he but touched the land,
And Paradise as in the prime,
  Was seen on every hand.

Receive him kindly to thy breast,
  O Earth for old love's sake,
For when alive thy beauties he
  More beautiful did make.

Harborne, October 28th. 1879.

NOVEMBER.

WINTER TOKENS.

WRITTEN FOR MY OLD FRIEND, HARRISON WEIR.

WHEN the stormcock blows his whistle,
  And the tomtit files his saw,
And the robin pipes his treble,
  And the rook flies with the daw,
And the cricket tunes his fiddle
  To the kettle's merry song,
And the sleety blast is driving
  The poor beggar-boy along ;
When the sea-coal fire burns brightest
  And the kittens loudest purr,
And no music to the sportsman
  Beats the pheasant's sudden whirr ;

When the cowherd sets his springles
  By the runnel and the mere,
And the starlings seek the plashets
  At the belling of the deer ;
When the throstle in the coppice
  Cracks his snails upon the stone,
And the carrion-crow sits telling
  His doleful tale alone,
While young colly* in the thicket
  Tries his notes o'er for the Spring,

---

* The Blackbird.

Q

And the wild geese, flying V-like,
  Speed swifter on the wing :

When the wild colt on the moorland
  A thicker jacket wears,
And the woodman to his cottage
  His biggest faggot bears ;
When the thatcher beats his smocket
  As the cutting "easter" blows,
And the postman wears the purple
  On his winter-bitten nose ;
And the old tup by the hedgerow
  Sets his back against the wind,
A sure token that the tempest
  Is only just behind :

When the flails make merry music
  To the urchins out of school,
And the old men seek the settle
  While the maidens card the wool ;
When fair Nelly from the forest
  Calls the acorn-hunting swine,
With her cheery " Chuggy, chuggy,"
  In the glow at even-chime,
And old gossips croon their stories
  As they knit around the fires,
And wee Jenny Wrens a-peeping
  See the poachers set their wires :

When Hodge, the weary plough-boy,
  Snores, with heavy head awry,
As Roger plays the sweetheart
  To prim Polly, rushing by,
While " Pedler Joe " laughs, spilling
  The cider in his mirth,
O'er Shep the farm-dog, dozing
  And dreaming on the hearth,
And the goodwife rocks the cradle
  Till the master's voice is heard—
" To bed, boys," as " Tuwhit, Tuwhoo,"
  Hoots sage Minerva's bird :

When the black storms shake their mantles
  O'er the leaf-forsaken trees,
And the snipe comes with the woodcock
  And the culvers seek the leas,
And the little lads are busy
  Making ready for the fray,
With their cannon, logs, and crackers,
  For great " Guy Fawkes his day "—
While piles of blazing bonfires
  And spiteful, hissing toys,
As serpents, squibs, and rockets,
  Please large and lesser boys ;

When the skylarks flock together
  And the linnets crowding sing,

And the children, 'mid the heather,
   Their red rose berries string :—
Then, the fruits all safely hoarded,
   Lo, the farmer waits for morn,
With a shout for bleak November
   And the merry hunter's horn,
While the dormouse and the squirrel,
   Curling cosy in their nest,
Tell of merry Christmas coming
   And a weary earth at rest.

DECEMBER.

THE BLESSED CHRISTMAS TIME.

Hark ! to the merry making-chimes,
   There is a blessing in the sound,
Bequeath'd us by the good old times,
   So let their greeting pass around.
" A merry Christmas to you, friend,
   Hang holly berries on your wall,
A sign the holy angels send,
   God's peace and comfort unto all."

That's right, ye ringers, pull away
   Until the hollow belfry rings ;
Each bell is wild with joy to-day,
   As to and fro it loudly sings—

" Christ's blessing be upon the poor,
  Ye rich your wealth to you is given,
Give, and be blessèd evermore :
  There is no poverty in Heaven."

The very air is sweet with love,
  As if bright seraphs on the wing,
Fresh from their fragrant homes above,
  O'er the white earth were hovering,
And on its sordid, selfish race
  Were breathing a celestial spell,
And calling up the glow and grace
  Our nature wore ere Adam fell.

There is no need for broken hearts,
  No need that any starving die,
If merchants driving to their marts
  Would look around with Christ-like eye,
Would dry the lonely widows' tears,
  Would help the helpless in their woe,
Make one long Christmas of their years,
  And so begin their Heaven below.

Ring louder, and yet louder ring
  Your happy bells, ye merry men,
More play, and let them wider swing,
  Hard hearts are growing soft again.

Old Mammon totters on his throne,
    The golden bands that held him there
Are melting—let him fall alone—
    God's love is reigning everywhere.

A smile is seen on Famine's cheek,
    A joyous gleam in blinded eyes ;
The deaf and dumb both hear and speak,
    And songs are heard instead of sighs.
Ring louder, and yet louder ring,
    There 's Heaven's own music in the strain ;
Oh that the world would ever sing—
    Glory to God, goodwill to men.

SHADOWS.

" The flowers live by the tears that fall
From the sad face of the skies ;
And life would have no joys at all
Were there no watery eyes."

Love thou thy sorrow ; grief shall bring
Its own excuse in after years ;
The rainbow ! see how fair a thing
God hath built up of tears.

HENRY SUTTON.

SHALL WE EVER MEET AGAIN?

" SHALL we ever meet again
    In the woodland by the sea ?
Will the moment bringing pain,
To the heart and to the brain,
    Come again to thee and me ?
Shall we hear again the moaning
    Of the ocean to the shore ?
Like the passionate intoning
    Of a devotee, Lenore,—
Shall we ever meet again ?
    Ah me ! that joy should borrow
A thorn to wound the heart
    From the pale red-rose of sorrow !
Adieu ! for we must part."

" We may never meet again
    In the woodland by the sea,

But the song, with the refrain,
Which we sang beside the main,
 Will be ever dear to me.
There is **no** sun that shineth
 But hath **its** spot **of** shade,
The brightest day declineth,
 And sweetest blossoms fade,
We may never meet again.
  Ah me ! **that love** should borrow
A thorn to wound **the** heart
 From the pale red-rose of sorrow !
Adieu ! for we must **part."**

Published by T. Murby, 32, Bouverie Street, London.

THE SUMMERS LONG AGO.

SONG.

Oh for those merry, **merry times,**
 When England's pleasant **vales**
Were musical with May-morn **chimes**
 And songs of nightingales !
When kingcups **smiled** through early dew
 And daisies loved **to** blow,
The sweet and sunny times **we knew**
 In summers long ago.

Oh wearisome and dreary days,
  Oh cold and blighting air !
Where are the olden roundelays
  That lightened half our care ?
The cuckoo is a silent bird,
  To sing the lark is slow,
Oh for the warbling that we heard
  In summers long ago !

The youth forsakes the trysting stile ;
  The maid forgets her vow ;
And minstrels pine to see the smile
  That Nature lacketh now.
Are love and song to die ? Alas !
  Shine, sun, with golden glow,
And give the glory, as we pass,
  Of summers long ago !

IN SOLITUDE.

SONG.

'Tis the weary West wind sighing
  In the lonely willow-tree,
Willow bare, whose leaves are lying,
Where benighted curlews flying,
  Wail most wistfully.

Sweet the melancholy moan
Of its murmuring undertone,
Lingering in that tree so **lone,**
   Sad as it may be.
'Tis the weary West wind sighing
   In the lonely willow-tree,
Willow bare, whose leaves are lying,
Where benighted curlews flying,
   Wail most wistfully.

Making melody for Sorrow
   In her solitary hour,
Who a charm will **often borrow**
For the anguish of the morrow,
   From a simple flower ;
Sigh, O sigh, thou Western wind,
Solace of the lonely mind,
Fellowship in thee I find,
   Spirit-soothing power.
'Tis the weary West wind sighing
   In the lonely willow tree,
Willow bare, whose leaves are **lying,**
Where benighted curlews flying,
   Wail most wistfully.

OUT OF THE DEPTHS.*

SONG.

**DEDICATED TO SAMUEL PLIMSOLL, ESQ., M.P., AND SET
TO MUSIC BY A. SCOTT GATTY.**

IT was the seaman's parting morn,
  Our white wing'd craft flew o'er the bay—
" Farewell " had spoke the skipper's horn
  To those who on the shore will stay—
And watch the less'ning vessel die,
And weeping sob the last " Good bye."

When lo ! a cloud upon the line
  That bounds the hardy sailor's view,
The meeting of the sky and brine,
  A cloud that leadens all the blue,
Till, " Storm ahead ! reef every sail "
Is heard aloud, " A gale ! a gale ! "

With deadly sweep throughout the deep,
  The wild rack rushes on,
And brave old tars, with tempest scars,
  Look sadly woe begone,
For 'mid the storm's loud roar and din
  The sea is madly rushing in.

---

* Published by Boosey and Co., 295, Regent Street, W.

"A leak ! a leak !" the pumps are mann'd,
   And hoping on against despair,
We toil away, a gallant band,
   Until is heard the hurried pray'r
As suddenly the ship goes down,
A coffin only made to drown !

Out of the depths arose a cry !
   A wail that smote the Nation's ears,
Until the land heav'd with a sigh,
   And strong men weeping bitter tears,
Broke forth at length, " O Lord how long ? "
And crush'd the foul and deadly wrong.

I WOULD I HAD SOMEONE TO LOVE.

SONG.

Oh had I a heart I could prize !
   I feel I am shorn of a wing ;
I envy the clouds in the skies
   As the larks soar towards them and sing.
The shore is the bride of the sea ;
   The hawk has his mate, and the dove ;
No lonely one happy can be ;
   I would I had someone to love !

Oh had I a hand I **could** press !
  An ear that would **list** to my tale ;
A bosom to share my distress,
  But wishing will nothing avail.
I yearn for a life with my kind,
  As the stars woo the **planets** above ;
Each heart for a heart was designed ;
  I would I had someone to love.

December **17th, 1870.**

————

THE TWO PRIMROSES.

Two little fair and fragrant flowers
  With petals holding golden hearts ;
A present from my western bowers,
  But tell me why the tear-drop starts.

They are no pale **and sickly things**
  Half suffocated with **the mirk,**
But healthy as our English springs
  Whose zephyrs kiss the tasselled birk.

The lovely tint each floweret bears
  Has nothing like it here below ;
To me, the blossom ever wears
  The tinge of Heaven's divinest glow.

O tell me not how manifold
   The pleasures are that wealth can bring,
A flower to me is more than gold,
   And ever has a song to sing.

And could you hear the tender words
   These simple flowers are chaunting now,
Sweet pretty plaintive under-chords
   That give **a throbbing** to the brow ;

They'd tell you that a little grave
   Was all the garden that they knew,
And that **by** yonder Western-wave
   Fanned by the purest airs they grew ;

And how a gentle maid had sought
   And found them where the runnels play,
And from their native haunts had brought
   The nurslings in her love away ;

And with a soft and tremulous hand
   Had planted them upon the nest,
Of one flown to that far off land
   Where God's dear dovelings sweetly rest.

O world so black with foul disgrace !
   So cold, unfeeling and unkind,
Know, where a flower can find a place,
   Sweet love will not be far behind ;

And when we mourn our lost apart,
  To bring the dead and living near.
'Twill try with a magician's art
  A primrose with a hidden tear.

WINIFRED.

" Blue-bells and Robins' eyes,"
  Who cries, who cries,
" Blue-bells and Robins' eyes ? "
  A little maid with yellow hair,
    Peeping through a lattice pane,
  Rosy cheeked and free of care,
    Up the village lane.

" Poppy and pimpernel
  Sort well, dames tell."
" Poppy and pimpernel,"—
  Sang a maiden half asleep,
    Woe-begone, and spirit torn,—
" Pimpernel, in pity weep ;
    Poppy, lull till morn."

" Boyslove is maiden's woe."
  Who sighs, Ho ! Ho !
" Boyslove is maiden's woe ? "

R

A damsel in the morning grey,
In simple cottagers' attire,
To a laddie in the May
By a fragrant briar.

" **Heartsease** and white rose,"
Death comes, **eyes** close,
" Heartsease and white rose."
In her grave the maid doth **rest** ;
Broken is her heart **of love** ;
The cold, cold clay upon her breast,
Evergreens above.

A DIRGE.

A BALLAD OF THE SEVERN.

" SWEET Severn's banks are broad and fair,
And fair the Severn's tide.
Sweet Severn's banks are broad and fair,
But I am almost in despair ;
So, Willie, Willie, O beware,
And shun the Severn's side.

To day in yonder westering sun
I saw the dead man's eye,
To day in yonder westering sun—

The cold, blind, doom-foreboding sun.
Now, mark those clouds, weird, dense, and dun ;
  There's evil in the sky."

On Severn's banks all broad and fair
  Are gathered Severn's pride.
On Severn's banks so broad and fair,
In sunny groupings here and there,
Meet many a young and joyous pair,
  At pleasant eventide.

And in and out, and round about
  Love-link'd with winsome glance ;
All in and out, and round about,
Like sunbeams darting through the rout,
With many a merry bound and shout,
  The happy couples dance.

When lo, a maiden's scream and splash
  Beside a golden willow !
O fearful scream ! O fatal splash !
Again, O wild and headlong dash,
For true love counteth nothing rash ;
  He buffets with the billow !

" O Willie !" Nothing more spake *she*,
  On rolled the Severn's wave,
So bright, so calm, so peacefully,

So bright, so calm, so peacefully,
And swift, that if aught uttered *he*,
  'Twas spoken in their grave.

Sweet Severn's banks are broad and fair,
  But, O its placid tide !
That placid tide so deep and fair,
For, wild with sorrow and despair,
Two mothers, with their tear-steeped hair,
  Are wailing by its side.

" My Kattern ! O this woeful scene !
  In one short moment gone !
My darling, sixteen summers green !"
" I saw the dead man's eye yestreen."
"Just sixteen sunny summers green !"
  " My Willie ! O my son !"

Peace ! let them rest, young love with love,
  Beneath the golden willow ;
Peace ! let them rest, dead dove with dove,
For, if our sweetest dream be love,
In life, in death, below, above,
  What matters it the pillow ?

March 30th, 1869.

SUMMER SNOW.

O ! WONDROUS scene !
A moment since and all was green ;
Green leaves and grass, fresh fern and moss,
Save where outshone a golden boss
Of furze or broom, whose sunny light
Hides now beneath a veil of white.

How very strange
This beautiful and sudden change !
The sun at summer-noon hath fled ;
The flowers have found a wintry bed ;
Yes, e'en the hawthorn's fragrant snow
Has vanished for awhile below.

But oh, the peace
That reigns around ! The throstles cease
Their music in th' umbrageous wood,
And larks, whose late melodious flood
Of love and rapture fired the breast,
Sit mute within their meadow-nest.

'Tis passing sweet,
This restful silence, so replete
With holy lessons, as the small
And fragile crystals gently fall,
And softlier than the swan's-down lie,
Or lid upon a seraph's eye.

What does it teach ?
The lovely scene doth ever preach
Of purity, to age and youth ;
And this sweet soul-consoling truth,
That e'en our sins, that crimson show,
Our God can whiter make than snow.

THE UNSEEN HAND.

A TREE that graced the western height
 Which bound the fading view,
Had caught the coming of the night
 With its funereal hue.
The dying day was breathing low ;
 The moon stood watching by ;
A pallor tinged the afterglow ;
 The south-wind was a sigh.

And thought went wandering where the waves
 Crept up a windy shore,
Hard by a row of little graves,
 Which I may see no more.
When lo, a soft and tiny hand
 My fingers did entwine ;
Yet, strange, around the sombre land
 There was no form but mine.

Barlow's Road, 1870.

A SIGH FOR SPRING.

SONG.

HARK ! how weirdly sounds the wind
  In the woodlands sighing !
And the whinneying o' the hind
  As the day is dying.
Heaven is but a watery waste ;
  Earth a desert dreary ;
Hither Spring, and prithee, haste,
  Come, for I am weary.

Pledges sweet of brighter days
  Are thy mornings vernal ;
Ante-pasts of love and praise
  In the land supernal :
Winter has a hoary pate,
  And a visage eerie ;
Friend of the disconsolate,
  Come, for I am weary.

O ! to see thy face again,
  And thy steps to follow—
Up the hill, and o'er the plain,
  And through hawthorn-hollow !
Listening to thy well-known voice,
  Ringing loud and cheery ;
" Mortals sigh not, but rejoice,
  Weep no more a-weary."

1879.

A SONG OF LONG AGO.

Iᴛ is a song of long ago,
  I heard a maiden sing;
And as she sang her tears did flow,
  As from a purling spring:
Its burden was the old, old tale,
  Of one who sat and mourn'd,
As plaintive as an autumn gale,
  Of passion unreturned;
And though full many a year had fled
  Since then of joy and woe,
Yet still she crooned, while tears were shed,
  That song of long ago.

"O why did gracious Heaven decree
  The heart to suffer bane,
And poison life's felicity
  With love that will not wane?
From dawn until the day doth close
  No light of joy I see,
Each Summer brings a canker-rose,
  The only bloom for me:
I loved; he did not love again,
  O! why this cup of woe?"
Alas! the bitter barren strain,
  That song of long ago.

Her mother's **fairest flower was she,**
  Her father's pride and joy,
And comely, **brave,** and good was **he**
  Who did her peace destroy :
He loved another, but his fate
  Was to **be chid and spurned,**
Nor did he **seek another mate,**
  Though **one towards him yearned.**
O ye who know the bliss of those
  Whose lives **with love o'erflow,**
Sing, when ye **meet** love's blighted **rose,**
  This song of long ago.

June 18th, 1880.

THE MESSAGE FROM THE SEA.

SONG.

ALL night, the wild tumultuous main
  With loud and angry **roar,**
Had strove to **dash the bark, in vain,**
  On Baggy's deadly shore ;
But at the breaking of the day,
She rode triumphant in the bay.

As midships the bold skipper stood,
  And the mad breakers eyed,

Which leapt like furies o'er the flood,
  He slapp'd the good ship's side,
And swore, by all he held most dear,
With her he nothing had to fear.

He was the foremost in the prow
  Upon her gala day,
When the fair figure on her bow
  First kiss'd the briny spray,
And his brave heart with pride beat high,
As like a bird he felt her fly.

" Hurrah ! hurrah ! she rides it well ; "
  The sturdy landsmen sing,
While plunging in the seething swell
  They mark her labouring ;
And as by Morte she ploughs her way,
" Heaven send her safe," the watchers pray.

Another night, a starless sky,
  A levin-lighted sea,
And near the dawn a crash and cry,
  The good ship, where is she ?
The waif-strewn beach is white with foam,
Where anxious waiters early roam.

When glistening in the bladder-wrack,
  Just thrown on Northam's strand,
They saw, with many a star and crack,
  A bottle on the sand,—

Which a young fisher-lad, for play,
Kick'd thoughtlessly along his way.

" Hold hard my boy," an old man cried,
    A weather-beaten tar,
As he a tiny scroll espied
    Beside a stranded spar,
While a young maiden, flushed with fear,
Stood half in dread the news to hear.

Then turning to the girl said he
  " ' For Polly, with my love,'
It is a message from the sea,
    Which sad to thee will prove,
And thus it reads, ' Just going down,
Brig, Betsy, Captain, Caleb Brown,' "

When she beside the seething bay,
    Dropt dead upon the shore ;
And now a phantom haunts for aye
    The sands of Appledore,
Which mariners oft see in white,
And sigh " Poor Polly walks to night."

THE MOURNER.

Down westward on a windy hill
  A lonely weeper stands,
While burning tears, that sad-eyes fill,
  Drop on her folded hands;

For the small hillock at her feet,
  Holds evermore the gem
Of all affection held complete—
  In life's fair diadem.

Alas! that the destroyer, Time,
  Such ruthless haste should make
To eat the stone and graven rhyme,
  Made hallowed for *her* sake;

And hence the mourner, bending there,
  Like one in form to pray,
Attempts the ruin to repair,
  Ere she pursues her way.

O! sore and weary must her heart
  Be in the silence now,
As sighing on that spot apart
  She weeps with throbbing brow—

Beside the monument fond care
   Had placed above *her* head,
Half razed by Desolation's share
   To make *her* doubly dead.

But let us plant anew the flowers,
   Where dock and darnel grow,
Such acts make sweet life's bitter hours,
   And steal away our woe.

Harborne, October 22nd, 1879.

ON ISCA'S BANK.

SONG.

" On Isca's bank the grass is green,
   And there the fairest flower is seen ;
By Isca's stream there sings a bird,
   A sweeter never branches stirred ;
Bloom flower, sing merry bird in tree,
   My Lilibell is all to me."

On Isca's bank a wail is heard ;
By Isca's stream there pipes no bird ;
   The snow is lying on the hill,
And there alone one lingers still,
Ah welladay ! sing welladay !
   Sweet Lilibell has passed away.

THE BLACK COUNTRY RAGGED FEAST.

YE who see in want a foe,
Ye who weep o'er others' woe,
Seeking early, seeking late,
How to bless an evil fate,
Know how good it is to see
Something of Humanity ;
This I saw at Kinverdale,
Listen to my truthful tale.

Once upon a summer day
Charity was heard to say,
" Pleasant is this home of ours,
Sweet the fields, the woods, and flowers,
But the whole would brighter seem
Did I realise my dream ;"
So she asked the ragged band
To enjoy her sunny land.

From the slag and from the slime,
From the gutter and the grime,
Hard of heart, with rude rebuffs,
Curses, kicks, and savage cuffs ;
Out from Squalor's reeking hut,
Factory, forge, and stagnant " cut,"
Stretching through long wastes of spoil,
Heaped by human ants of toil :

On they came, mute, halt and lame,
Odd, droll things without a name,
Save Nipperkin—a word for small,
Which seemed to serve them one and all.
Some too very gaunt and thin,
Foul without and black within,
Ghostly, grim, and hollow of cheek,
Blind and barefoot, weary and weak.

Natives of our English land,
There they were—an outcast band,
Come from dingy dens of crime,
Little old folk before their time ;
And, oh ! 'twas a sad sight to see
Such tiny wrecks of misery,   .
Little six years led by seven,
Getting their first glimpse of heaven.

Some with ears that never heard
Music from a forest bird,
Little cheeks that never smiled,
So imbruted was the child ;
Eyes that never skyward glanced,
Little feet that never danced,
Little hands ne'er raised in prayer,
Little hearts o'erfull of care.

Little mites of waifs and strays,
With their strange unchildish ways,
Nestled in the lap of sin,
Criminals their only kin ;
Stunted things from grimy deeps,
Where the gorgon Danger keeps,
And black Horror often stands,
Terror-struck, with lifted hands.

Little **maidens,** too, were there,
Little pale things—famine-fair ;
Souls like little blighted flowers,
Yet as dear to God as ours ;
And I asked, **as** there I stood,
In a half-complaining mood,
As the **frail** things toddled by,
" **If they** perish, why not I ? "

Living thus from day **to day,**
Knowing nought of healthful play,
Bred in regions dense with glooms,
Poisoned **by hot** furnace-fumes,
Where Destruction's teeth are seen
Eating up each blade of green,
And the only skies they view
Wear a red or murky hue ;

Blind to every virtuous deed,
None to teach them, none to lead,
Ignorant of the world above,
Strangers to that sweet word—love :
Who can marvel that they try
Which can cheat the most and lie ?
And since hunger must be fed
Sometimes steal a crust of bread ?

God be thanked for hands to guide,
Hearts whose duty is their pride,
And the blessed Sabbath-break,
Hallowing the weary week ;
For amid the slough and slime
Ringing with the holy chime,
Voices now are heard to say,
" Hither is the better way."

Blessings be upon your deed,
Ye who help the sons of need,
Visiting from door to door,
Seeking out the little poor.
This the Heavenly Master did,
Children to His presence bid ;
" Those who do the same," saith He,
" Will have done it unto Me."

s

THE GRAVE ON THE HILL

WE stood beside a little grave,
   Wrapt in a robe of white,
And where the horse-hoofed chestnuts wave,
   A minstrel met our sight.
When listening with attentive ear,
   Just like a plaintive song,
And tender as a mother's tear,
   Thus spoke his pleading tongue :

"Say shall these pretty dovelings lie
   All lonely in their nest,
Without a tear, without a sigh,
   Forsaken and unblest ?
Good strangers for the love of those
   Who laid their darlings here,
I pray you spare a young year's rose,
   Or Flora's frozen tear."

He pleaded so, that ere we left
   That grave upon the hill,
For love of those poor hearts bereft
   A white winged daffodil,
A tiny drop of living snow—
   We on the hillock laid,
And to the sleeping babes below
   Our reverent homage paid.

February 22nd, 1877.

A MAY-SHADOW.

A COTTAGE in a winding lane,
  Reed-roofed and clasped with jessamine ;
A face seen through a window-pane
  With charms that any lad would win.

A pair of eyes, as sapphire blue ;
  A rivulet of golden hair ;
Cheeks shaming e'en the rose's hue ;
  Fresh vermeil lips of beauty rare.

A morning in the month of May ;
  A laddie standing at the gate ;
A look, but not a word to say ;
  A sigh from one without a mate.

A little chamber, hawthorn sweet ;
  A head low resting on a hand ;
Slow pacing of two dainty feet ;
  A vacant stare out on the land.

A tiny drop of liquid pearl ;
  A joy gone nothing can restore ;
The funeral of a village girl ;
  A grave, and peace for evermore.

TO MY SON ON THE LOSS OF HIS LITTLE DAUGHTER MILLY.*

Son of mine ! to see thee weep,
   Opes a wound I dreamt had healed,
And the woe I thought asleep,
   Wakes, and will not be concealed,

For again among the dead,
   I am called to take my place ;
By your little darling's bed ;
   Milly, pretty babe o' grace.

Lay her in her little nest,
   And let this thy comfort be,
What the Father does is best :
   Time has taught this truth to me.

Who can tell the evil she
   Might have suffered and have seen ?
No prevision, son, have we,
   And life is as it hath been.

Meeting means but parting here ;
   Parting meeting far above ;
Plant the willow, drop the tear,
   But remember God is Love.

---

* Died August 31st, 1875, and buried in Saltley Churchyard,
Warwickshire.

THE PILOT'S STORY.

You ask for the " City of London," sir :—
Do you see that tug there ?—that is her !
And Kingston—the master, I am the man,
And you want me to speak of the wreck, as I can ?

I've little to say, sir, yet what I know
Of the " Northfleet's " loss and that night of woe,
I will give to you in my own rough way,
Though sailors can *do* much better **than** *say*.

We had just brought up where the pilots lie,
As the stinging sleet went driving by ;
And hard after that came a hazy rain ;
The stars had been out, but were in again ;

When we saw a big blaze off Dungeness,
A look—and we knew that it meant distress.
" Up with the anchor, my lads," cried I,
As a shower of rockets burst in the sky.

And steering away where the fires burn'd blue,
The luckless vessel soon hove in view,
As her riding-light in the foremast shroud
Was sinking, so " Ship ahoy !" aloud

I shouted : I saw she was going down,
And knew that many a one must drown,
For souls by hundreds were struggling there
In all the agony of despair.

In less than the time I've been talking to you
We were all among them. Says I to my crew,
" For God's sake, into the boat ! be brave,
And see how many, lads, you can save."

For a moment I lost my head and legs,
Since they crowded around me as thick as eggs.
" Hold hard ! " I thunder'd, " and let her drive,"
For the sea with the drowning was all alive.

Well, we pick'd up thirty-four ; but hold—
No, thirty-eight, if the truth be told ;
For their boat that was sinking beneath my view
Had four of my own good sturdy crew.

That poor little thing, the Cap'n's wife,—
I'm happy to say I sav'd her life,
And huddled her into my berth below :
Says she, " Is my husband alive or no ? "

I answer'd, with look as hard as steel,
" Gone off in a lugger, and safe at Deal."
May God forgive me for telling the lie,
But what could I say ? so that said I.

And then she pray'd as a woman, sir, will,
That I through the night would keep a watch still ;
I promis'd, and did, though a mad **chopping sea**
Oft threatened to make a shark's meal o' **me.**

And what **did we see at the peep o'** the day ?
The three **mast-tops** sticking **up in the bay,—**
When we very soon made us **a hasty flight,**
To save the poor wretches the pain **of the** sight.

To **finish my** tale, and **to cut it short,**
We put on all steam **and got into port :**
" Is **the** Cap'n **all** right **?" and the** answer **came,**
     " No "—
That was a regular knock-**down** blow.

I blubbered just like a silly child,
For the **poor little** young thing **I knew was** wild.
" You are **wanted,"** someone said, **" below ;**
The skipper's wife "—but I dare not **go.**

For **she,** poor broken-hearted soul,
Her sorrow was quite beyond control ;
She would neither bite **a** bit nor sup,
Though I got some tea and made her a cup,—

Made her a cup with these very same hands.
Ay, a loss like o' that, sir, who understands ?
But if ever again we meet together,
I hope it will be in better weather.

You've heard what the bos'n and Pilcher said,
And seen how Jack Stanley went off to their aid,
When the Spaniards who sank them had left them
    to die,
With never a speck of a star in the sky.

Curse the pirates ! I say ; and, egad !
If I'd got them here, I'd hang them, my lad ;
I'd string them all up from stern to stem,
And make a jolly quick end o' them.

Hear poor Cap'n Knowles—pray pardon the tear—
" Save the women and children : *my* duty is here."
" A Briton," you say : you'd have done the same :
It is easy to die if you are but game.

Good skippers think nought of themselves, sir,
    when
They're sinking with children, women and men ;
And the " Northfleet's "—God bless him for losing
    his life—
Had only been married six weeks to his wife.

'T is well for the hulk that the coast was clear,
And no British thunderer chanced to be near,
Or a shot would have made her move more slow,
And sent her down to her place below.

I mean the " Murillo " !—the murderous fox,
She thought to get off, but she's safe in the docks,
Our seadogs have just haul'd her in from the main
With the blood on her bows, like the brand upon
    Cain.

I'm ashamed, I say, sir, to pipe my eye,
But the heavens were rent with their drowning cry ;
And English sailors, though rough we may be,
Have the old true stuff of humanity.

I have little to tell, as I said before ;
I have done a man's duty, and nothing more ;
The help that we lent them, alas ! was small,
But I would to God we had sav'd them all.

LOVE IN SHADOW.

Peace, weary heart, forget to love ;
  Hope, plume no more thy silken wings ;
My passion, like a widow'd dove,
  In solitary places sings :
The brightest visions of the soul,
  The warmest raptures of delight,
And joys unfettered by control,
  Must vanish in the shades of night.

Bid not again the roses bloom,
　　Which shed their odour on my way ;
Let not the sun my path illume,
　　Nor forest songsters charm the day :
The soul that has no living power
　　To move a human heart should dwell
Forgotten, like a withered flower,
　　And silent as a shattered bell.

Oh, cherish not the olden dreams !
　　The past is fled, and memory
Is like the moon whose fitful gleams
　　Fall on a dark and troubled sea ;
Chant not again the gladsome lays
　　That made my young emotions move :
I sigh not for departed days,
　　And am too weary now for love.

HOLLY AND MISTLETOE.

Holly and mistletoe,
　　Coral and pearl,
Set in rich emerald,
　　Bought for my girl—
Bought for my pretty one,
　　Oh ! how her eyes,
Joyous with sparkles,
　　Will flash with surprise !

Holly and mistletoe !
  What—do I dream ?
Where are her little orbs
  Lit with love's gleam ?
Where are the tiny feet
  Dancing around ?
Bright eyes and nimble feet !
  Where ?—underground.

Holly and mistletoe,
  Visions divine,
Tender and beautiful,
  Come where ye shine !
Visions of little lips
  Sweeter than sweet ;
Safe from the snow-storm now,
  Safe from the sleet.

Holly and mistletoe,
  Coral and pearl,
Red for the rosy cheeks
  Worn by my girl ;
White for the fairest face
  Nature e'er drew ;
Green for the memory
  Love keepeth new.

Holly and mistletoe,
  Crowning her name,

Welcome for her sweet sake,
Welcome each game—
" Truckle the trencher," and
" Kiss in the ring,"
" Apple and candle," " Buff,"
" Courtier and king."

Holly and mistletoe,
Yes, I am blest,
Merry-mass comes, and lo !
I am possessed :
Up goes the kissing-bush,
Down cometh she,
Singing " Sweet merry-mass,"
Ever to me.

Holly and mistletoe,
Tears must be shed ;
Ye have your living ones,
I have my dead ;
Yours is a present joy,
Mine is a past ;
Clear is your sky of life,
Mine overcast.

Holly and mistletoe,
Long may it be,
Friends, ere my loneliness
Ever you see ;

But if that time shall come,
  Then you will know
More of my text than my
  Sermon can show.

THEY BID ME LOVE AND SMILE AGAIN.

They bid me love and smile again,
  As in the days gone by ;
And new love driveth old love's pain,
  They tell me when I sigh.
But oh ! my spirit hath a wound
  No art of love can heal !
My antidote's beneath the mound
  Where hearts aye cease to feel.

I met thee in the happiest time
  That youthful souls can meet,
When May was in her maiden-prime,
  And everything was sweet ;
When throstles with their loudest notes
  Trilled out their joy in song ;
And little linnets tuned their throats
  With love the whole day long.

We parted, ere the summer came
  With blithe and rosy June ;
While yet the cuckoo sung his name
  To merry merles at noon ;
And oh ! the loss that parting made
  Is only known to me.
Dost mind thy promise in the glade ?—
  Still love forgiveth thee.

OH, THE HEART HATH ITS TREASURES.

OH, the heart hath its treasures, deep hid in the grave,
  The forms that it loved in the heyday of youth,
And the true and the tender will evermore crave
  A glimpse of those pictures Hope painted for Truth :
How they dwell in the memory ! fair and divine
  As the moon's rounded pearl on the bosom of Night,
Or happy old age, in its peaceful decline,
  With its time-honoured beauty enchanting the sight.

As the traveller turns on his heel to behold
  The bloom of the landscape that purples the view,
Deep tinging the distance of russet and gold,
  Where the lips of his loving ones uttered adieu ;
So the soul in her loneliness looks to the past
  For comfort to solace her wearisome way,
As the wail of the winter comes loud on the blast,
  And the glow of the sunset departs with the day.

LAYS
FOR THE LITTLE ONES.

The Children of Old England
   With little merry eyes,
Who light the home with sunshine,
   And make our Paradise !
Not blither sing the birdies
   That nestle in the corn,
Than they when Joy's own ditties
   They warble at the morn.

THE DUCKLING.

Old Mother Cubidee went for a walk,
  With her seven little chickens and one little duck,
Amusing them all with her old-fashioned talk,
  Clickity, clackity, clock, cluck, cluck,—

Till she came to a pool by the side of a road,
  With her seven little chickens and one little duck,
When ducky plunged in where the water was broad,
  Clickity, clackity, clockity, cluck.

The hen she looked on with her little ones near,
  The seven little chickens amazed at the duck,
Till she felt every feather a-quiver with fear,
  Clickity, clackity, clockity, cluck.

The little rogue floated around and around,
  Then stood on his head, did the wee little duck,
While the hen screamed aloud with despair in the sound,
  Clickity, clackity, clockity, cluck.

T

And now standing up on the water so deep,
  And flapping his winglets, the dear little duck,
He gave a loud laugh, then he took a wild leap ;
  Clickity, clackity, clockity, cluck.

His sport being over he paddled to land,
  As if it were nothing, the quaint little duck ;
When the hen gave a chuckle of joy to her band,
  Clickity, clackity, clock, cluck, cluck.

THE ORPHAN LAMB.

My pretty little gibby-lamb,
And has your Mamma gone
And left you here, my pretty dear,
All hungry and alone ?
O never mind it little pet
For I will love you well,
So when you want your dinner, dear,
Just ring your tiny bell,
And I will bring my basket full
Of nice and dainty meat—
Young butter-buds and tender grass,
And new milk, rich and sweet ;
Don't cry again my darling, dear,

Since your Mamma is dead,
I'll be your little mother now
And make your cosy bed,
And in the pleasant meadows, love,
So golden and so bright,
We'll play together all the day,
And kiss " Good-bye " at night.

TELL ME WHAT THE MILL DOTH SAY.

TELL me what the mill doth say,
Clitter, clatter, night and day ;
When we sleep, and when we wake,
Clitter, clatter, it doth make.
Never idle, never still,
What a worker is the mill !
Clitter, clatter, clitter, clatter,
What a worker is the mill.

Tell me what the rill doth say
As it trips along its way,
Sweet as skylark on the wing,
Ripple, dipple, it doth sing ;

Never idle, never still,
What a worker is the rill !
Ripple, dipple, ripple, dipple,
What a worker is the rill.

Listen to the honey bee
As he dances merrily
To the little fairy's drum,
Humming, drumming, humming, dum ;
Never idle, never still,
Humming, drumming, hum it will,
Humming, drumming, humming, drumming,
Humming, drumming, hum it will.

Like the mill, the rill, and bee,
Idleness is not for me,
What says cock-a-doodle-doo ?
" Up ! there's work enough for you ; "
If I work then with a will
It will be but playing still,
Ever cheery, never weary,
It will be but playing still.

THE SONG OF THE PEWIT.

I'M little Petawin Pewit,
  And live out on the moor,
In a pretty little grass house,
  With peat-turf for my door.
I can't sing like the thrushes,
  I often wish I could,
Nor warble like the linnets
  That live within the wood ;
But then I do the best I can,
  As mine have done before,
And gaily wave my graceful wing
  When speeding o'er the moor,
Singing ever as I fly,
 " Life is very sweet,
Pewit witity, pewit witity,
  Pewit, witityweet."

When comes the time for buttercups,
  And bluebells, in my nest
I sit amid the sedgy tufts
  And plume my shining breast ;
Or saying " Good-bye, darling,"
  Unto my little wife,
I pass the woods and meadows
  And lead a pleasant life—

In finding for our baby-birds
    The simple food they need,
Then hasten to my home again
    Rejoicing in my deed,
Singing ever as I fly,
    " Life is very sweet,
Pewit witity, pewit witity,
    Pewit, witityweet."

—

THE CHILD AND THE BUTTERFLY.

On the silvery white of a dewberry bloom,
Laden with sweets and delicious perfume,
The Queen of the summer, in glory arrayed,
Was resting awhile in the skirt of a glade,

When a bright little maid with a pretty blue eye,
The dear little fairy thing chanced to espy,
And the joy that it gave her will never be told,
As it folded its pinions of crimson and gold.

Then, smiling, the little one singing began,
" O butterfly ! butterfly ! spread out thy fan ;
The humming-bird's boast and the peacock's is thine,
Bright hues that the sapphire and ruby outshine.

Thy slender horns, beaded and pearly as dew,
Surmounted with jewels, enchanted I view,
As perched on that blossom, an airy-wing'd sprite,
I see thee now basking in sunshiny light.

O butterfly ! butterfly ! flit not away,
But just let me touch thee, my beauty, I pray ;
I'll do thee no harm pretty gem of the sky !
There !—now thou art flown, naughty creature,
    O fie ! "

THE SQUIRREL.

Up the ash, and down the oak,
    And through the hazel bushes,
Gliding where the ravens croak,
    And merry make the thrushes,—
Nought cares he what foes there be,
    One, or two, or many ;
He can climb the highest tree,
    Far away from any.

Pricking ears, with curling tail,
    In the fork* he sitteth ;
But if shouts do him assail,
    Far away he flitteth.

* Where two or more branches begin.

Nought cares he what foes there be,
He's the true wood-ranger ;
On he leaps from tree to tree
Ever out of danger.

THE DORMOUSE.

LITTLE dotty derrymouse,
Sleeping in your tiny house,
   Rounded like a **ball,—**
Pretty nest all made of sedge,
Hidden **now in thorny hedge,**
   Now in privet wall.

What is it you dream about,
Winter in and winter out,
   In your coat of brown ?
It must be of happy days
Spent in pleasant sunny **ways**
   Far away from **town.**

Little dotty derrymouse,
Sleeping in your cosy house,
   Though the storms may wail,—
Yet they never waken **you,**
Where you lie rolled **up from view,**
   Circled by **your tail.**

Now you ope your litle eyes,
What a look of mild surprise,
    Derrymouse I see.
Pretty creature **do not fear,**
For **no enemy is** near.
    Will you come with **me ?**

If you will, then in the spring,
With each sweet and juicy thing,
    I will see **you fed ;**
And when winter comes again,
Sheltered from the wind and rain,
    You shall make your bed.

Must you close again your eye ?
Bye ! **then, little dotty, bye !**
    And when fast asleep,
I **will wrap you** up so warm,
And from everything like harm
    Will my " derry " keep.

TO RUFUS, A PET CAT.

Rufus, Rufus, sitting there,
With thy philosophic air,
Gazing straight into the fire,
What is it doth thee inspire ?
Is thy catship wondering why
Cats were ever doomed to die
Since such cosy beds are thine,
Ottomans and sofas fine,
Couches, too, and rugs so dainty ;
Or is thy fond dream **of** plenty ?
Squatting there without a purr,
In thy nice **warm coat** of fur,
Making **never a** complaint,
Perfect picture of content,
Perched up on thy haunches fat,
What art thinking of old cat ?
Are thy thoughts about thy tail,
Which **was never known to fail,**
When in thy feline repose
Aye to curl around thy toes ?
Or art dreaming of the coals
And the suffering of poor souls
Now that brutal men have sold
Their humanity for gold,

Robbing mortals of that heat,
Necessary as their meat?
Prithee tell me what art thinking,
With thy emerald eye-balls blinking?
I would give a mite had we
No more need to cry than thee;
Hour by hour I see thee lie
Watched by every passer by,
No dread tyrant of a boy
Thee to torture or annoy,
Pampered pet of all the house,
Far too fat to catch a mouse.
Rufus when a cat I see,
Housed as happily as thee,
Then I know that bliss is near,
And a love that knows no fear.
Sweet cat-comfort then be thine,
While thy master, so benign,
And thy mistress joy to see
True domestic peace in thee.

THE ASS AND THE GEESE.

ONCE on a time some silly things,
  Well known as geese by their confession,
Went to a pond to wash their wings,
  Not thinking then to take possession,

Until a thirsty ass drew near,
  To take a cooling draught of **water,**
When lo ! a storm assailed his ear
  Of mingled **hiss** and cackling clatter.

" **Away !** " cried **one young** stupid thing,
  What right have you in our dominion ?"
And raising up her angry wing—
  When thus the Ass—" keep **down** your pinion.

I've toiled a life-time on this farm,
  You've spent your moments here on grazing,
Avaunt! or you will come to harm ;
  Your insolence is quite amazing."

Then in he stepped whilst they flew out,
  With deafening screams and fearful flutter,
Thus Folly's flock was put to rout,
  In terror that no words can utter.

———

THE DOLL'S LEVÉE.

A DOLL'S Levée ! **We all** have dolls,
  Of some particular **kind :**
Live Kates, or witching waxen Polls,
  To please the infant **mind.**

And so, this merry month of June,
  While everything is gay,
And nature sings her sweetest tune,
  We keep high holiday.

See, seated on her royal throne.
  The fair Macassarine ;
A lady all delight to own
  As Dolly's dimpled Queen.

And near her, with a noble air,
  In glittering armour dight,
Sir Bassinet protects the fair,
  A bold and stalwart knight.

While lovely maids, a brave array,
  In softest swansdown clad ;
And smiling, like the fields o' May,
  Make all our darlings glad.

In silken sashes, Scissoret,
  And Needleëtta view ;
Rose Ribbondene, and Cushionet,
  And coy Cottonia too.

Here, bright Celine, with sapphire eyes,
  And pearl drops in her ears,
There, Elfie, with a fay's surprise,
  In bridal robe appears ;

Next Thimbleleno, golden-haired,
    With **pert Prunelle**, the chit;
And Braidaline, as if she dared
    To rival Pinalit.

And now our little **ones** begin
    To gather in their joy;
With whom, to covet is no sin,
    When they behold a toy.

" O, **what a** little dear, mamma !"
    " **And I** should like him, too ; "
" **Pray buy** that lovely **boy, papa,**
    For your own **Totty, do** ! "

" 'Ook, **sissy, 'ook** !—O, I do 'ove
    That **pitty one** in white ! "
" If I'd **that** girl in **blue,** above,
    I **would** be good to night ! "

'Tis thus the prattle **of** their tongues
    Rings through the spacious Hall,
As tuneful as **the** merry songs
    At linnets' **festival.**

And, long as there are Nolls and Polls,
    With little pattering feet,
Some loving hand will dress the dolls,
    To make their joy complete.

A COMICAL STORY.

A TALL stalwart Fir, as he stood by the way,
Was heard by a traveller, passing one day,
In a sort of soliloquy, first it appears,
Then talking to one, who had leaves for his ears :
" I think it's myself, but I am not quite sure ; "
Much perplexed in his look, like a simpleton pure,
" Those leaves are the ivy's, and never my spikes ; "
I'm puzzled a little, like Timothy Tykes."
When out spoke the parasite : " Friend, you are mad :
What can you be else but an ivy, my lad ? "

Old Fir was confounded, and greatly amazed—
The picturé of one, whom we reckon as crazed,
He could not refute it, but still he said, " Sir,
I am not an ivy, I say, but a fir."
Pert Ivy, then bade him glance down at his feet,
With " Pray now confess, that you really are beat ;
For if you look closely, I think 'twill be found,
" I am Mister Ivy, right down to the ground."
" Tis true, and not true," said old Fir but I guess
That you'll find I'm the tree, and that you are the
    dress."

MORAL.

Thus falsehood will argue, and frequently try
To bury the Truth, in the garb of a lie.

Written in " Clovelly Hobby."

MERRILY THE MOMENTS FLY.

"Twoot, twoot, twoot,"
    The thrush sings in the tree ;—
"Twoot, twoot, twoot,"
    And not afraid is he ;
Hear him by the road-way side,
Morning, noon, and eventide,
Singing to each passer by
" Merrily the moments fly."

"Twink, twink, twink,"
    The chaffinch singeth now,
"Twink, twink, twink,"
    In yonder hazel bough ;
While the merry blackbirds' chime,
With the cuckoo's summer-rhyme,
Singing to each passer by,
" Merrily the moments fly."

"Tweet, tweet, tweet,"
    The little linnet sings ;
"Tweet, tweet, tweet,"
    As on the twig it springs,
Till the children welcome May,
Joining in the roundelay,
Singing, " Shout each passer by
Merrily the moments fly."

PATRIOTIC SONGS

AND OTHER POEMS.

No thought was there of dastard flight;
Linked in the serried phalanx tight,
Groom fought like noble, squire like knight.

SCOTT.

OUR OWN BELOVED ENGLAND.

Our own belovéd England,
  Our glory and our pride,
There is no land like England,
  In all the world beside.
We love her peaceful valleys,
  We love her breezy hills,
The music of her warblers,
  The murmur of her rills.
CHORUS.—Our own belovéd England,
  Our glory and our pride,
There is no land like England,
  In all the world beside.

U

We pray for all in England,
Of high and low degree,
And men of every Nation,
The bondman **and the free** ;
And long may England flourish,
And joy be with her seen ;
May peace **dwell** with the people,
And God preserve her Queen.
Chorus.—Our own belovéd England,
Our glory and our pride,
There is no land like England,
In all the world beside.

BULLER THE BRAVE.

WRITTEN ON THE OCCASION OF DEVON'S WELCOME **HOME TO**
HER HERO, COLONEL REDVERS BULLER, C.B., **V.C.**

Once more from the battle-field, **over** the wave,
To **the** home of the hero we welcome **the** brave,
With the Cross on his breast like a luminous **star,**
The eye of the Army, and soul of the War.

Isandula avenged, **and Intombi, where fell**
Our braves, **as** the savage **swooped** down with **a yell,**
Let Chelmsford be honoured ; but Buller's the boast
Of the honest old land, from its heart to **the coast.**

So we shared in his laurels, for Devon's dear sake,
As they did in the days of bold Grenville and
    Drake,
When Forbes, the intrepid, rode, breathless, to wire
His levin-like dash, in a message of fire.

At bloody Zlobani, though craggy and steep,
The red posts of peril he won at a leap,
Where a host at each turn bade the stoutest beware,
For his watchword was "Onward, and never Despair!"

Aye, bravest in danger, and first in the van,
A lion in courage, in feeling a man,
No comrade in arms could be struck by the foe,
But his prowess increased, as his pity would flow.

Yes, those who fought with him know best, and can
    tell
How he held the black tigers in check with his spell,
As he succoured the helpless that fell in the fray,
And bore them in pride, and in triumph away.

And when "To Ulundi," the order was given,
And the foe from his kraal and his covert was driven,
Our Buller, to counsel, was ever at hand,
The trust of his Chief, and the hope of his band.

And oh, if the wild Umvolosi could speak,
How he on his charger the torrent would break
When off like a leviner fleet, at a **bound**,
To scent out the slot, like a trusty old hound.

Now here and now there, over donga and drift,
Through mealies, steed-high, on the veldt, at the
    swift,
Or straight to the swamp, where the herbage **was**
    rank,
With danger in front, and with death on the flank.

Past the bush, where huge Pythons are lurking in
    coils,
Like living lianas, to snare in their toils,
Where light is a stranger, **or** sickly and green,
And dens where the desert-born lion is seen.

Just hear his brave words, **as he spins up a glen,**
His cheery old chirp to encourage **his men ;**
" Good, Bravo, my hearties, but mind, **have a** care,
Or Ketché may catch you.   Halloa boys ! a snare.—

" What ho, there ! **Ware hawk** : by Jack Russell, look
    out,
There's game up my lads, that is Beresford's shout,"
For a hiss as of serpents is heard in the grass,
And a thousand fierce savages block up the pass.

" Sit well in the saddle, and tighten the girth,
    Then off with a rush, like a storm at the birth,
    And as your proud chargers sweep on with a run,
    Set your sabres at play in the flash of the sun.

" Hurrah, lads ! we know that the enemy's there,
    To-morrow we'll have out the beast from his lair."
    And, sure as the day, he was true to his word,
    For the kranzes, and kloofs in the morning were
        stirr'd.

As they marched in the square, 'twas a picture to see
Bold Evelyn Wood,* with his lads all a-glee,
While Buller rode round where the rock-rabbits hide
And drew on the foe in the flush of his pride.

Anon from the heights, like the swarming of bees,
As red Sakabulas rush under the trees,
With plumes of grey scarlet, and skin-shields of
    white,
Dense hordes of wild Zulus are hasting to fight.

Now ringing us round, with a tumult like hell,
They blazed, as we answered with shot and with shell,
Yet spite, too, of assegais flying around,
Our tight little wall of men stuck to their ground.

---

* The following bit of information may interest the author's friends :—
Just after this poem was written, he was proud to make the very pleasing
discovery that on his mother's side the brave and gallant Sir Evelyn was
a kinsman ; he and the poet having descended from the same old Tiverton
stuck of Woods which produced the good and famous Sir Matthew, who
became twice Lord Mayor of London.

But the front of the foe becomes broken and jagged,
And his courage now falters that never had flagged,
· For each withering volley is mowing him down,
And his fortune at last is beginning to frown.

A pause—then a panic, when Evelyn Wood,
Dragoon and bold Lancer are off like a flood,
But not before Buller, the foremost in fight,
Sweeps out like a whirlwind, and puts him to flight.

Yet often the foe on that terrible day,
Turned round like a lion and kept them at bay,
As they in their onslaught compelled him to run,
Till Beresford shouted " Ulundi is won ! "

September 1st, 1879.

WATERLOO BOB.

A LITTLE wizen-visaged man
   Of eighty-three or more,
Who bends " two-double " as he leans
   Against his cottage door.

I love a hero from my heart,
   So hearing of his fame,
I drew towards him, shook his hand,
   And ask'd him for his name :

When smiling crowfeet graced each eye,
  Which sparkled like a star,
And, as I stood the vet'ran by,
  Thus spoke the man of war.

"**Wor** I at Waterloo? yo ask,
  I rather think I wos;
Yes, I remember Hugomont
  And bloody Quarterbros!

And for the little part I took
  In that tremenjus fray,
I gets from our most gracious Queen
  My eighteen-pence a day.

My krisen'd name? 'tis Robert Phipps,
  But heer at Harborne, sir,
Whene'er they calls for ' Little Bob,'
  I'm ' theer ' without demur.

Well, why they calls me so, I s'pose,
  Is reasonable, no doubt,
Within my shoes I'm five-foot-three,
  And five-foot-two when out.

A very little fellow, but
  In Boney's stirring days,
They worn't pertikler beowt the soize
  If **yo** had plucky ways.

Yo'd loike to heer a bit perhaps
　Of whot this lod has seen,—
And moind my mottor's ' Tell the truth '—
　To Paris I ha'e been.

I entered with the Grond Allies
　Jest arter Waterloo,
And, sir, yo shod ha'e seen our lods,
　And seen the Frenchies, too.

The duke and Blucher, they wor theer,
　Besoide the Rooshan King,
And daa'nt the sans culottes look queer
　To heer we British sing.

Old Boney would ha'e broke his heart
　If he had caught that sight ;
I pitied him ; I seen him once ;
　'Twor jest befowr the fight.

I knew him by the three-cock'd hat,
　And green coat that he wore,
Grey cloak, white breeches, boots and spurs,
　But never saw him more.

The battle then had not begun,
　At least I saw no soigns,
When he afore his Curraseers
　Rode up and down the loines.

I never shall forget the sound
  Of welcome which they gave
To cheer him, but their stonding ground
  Wos very soon their grave :—

For with a heavy, thundering boom
  Our guns began to play,
And many a brave mon met his doom
  On that too fatal day.

I saw the duke of Brunswick fall,
  Sir Thomas Picton, too ;
The bugle made a deadly call
  That day at Waterloo.

What did I do ? the best I could
  To stave the Frenchman's shock,
Stood upright, sir, and down-straight, so,
  Jest like old six o'clock.

Our reg'ment wos the forty-fourth,
  All little fellows we,
And Wellington this message sent,
  By's aidekong,—d'ye see ?

' The General orders yo to bear
  Those colours from the field,
For yo're too weak to hold'em, men ;'
  We were too *strong* to yield.

'What say yo boys?' our Kurnel ask'd,
  '*Where'er they go, we go,*'
Sez brave O'Malley, 'Tell the duke
  That all my men say 'NO!'

'**Rank** Mutiny!' old "Hookey" said,
  But they're a gamey lot,
So let them have their way and lose
  Their colours and be shot.'

We were but lods, and very small,
  But how we fought that day
Against old Boney's Granadeers
  The figgirs, sir, will say.

Full seven hunderd we went in,
  We came out thirty-three,
And shot to ribbons wos our flag
  Amid the devilry.

To save the pole had been enough,
  We sav'd the rag besoide,
The Frenchman cut up very rough,—
  No, sir, I hav'n't loied.

I've told my story straight as truth,
  My chum was first to fall;
A soldier's head ain't bullet-proof
  Against a cannon **ball.**

And our O'Malley, bold as true,
  Wos wounded in the foight;
But, though we won the victory,
  It **wor a** horrid soight."

This living hero of the ranks
  Was sorely stricken, too;
So here I give a Briton's thanks
  To Bob of Waterloo.

THE CLARION SOUNDS!

THE clarion sounds! uprouse! awake!
  There's tempest in the air,
The muttering clouds already break,
  With anger brooding there.
O Britain, **dost thou not behold**
  War's portent in the sky?
Arise! thy place is with the bold;
  We must be free or die!

The clarion sounds! and **on** the heights,
  And in the valleys green,
With banners from a thousand fights,
  A dauntless host is seen;

They gather in the tented field,
 And raise their standard high ;
A **band** that knows not when to yield ;
 We must be free or die !

The clarion sounds ! again, again !
 And hark ! the rolling drum :—
We'll keep a look-out on the main,
 And he **who dares, may come.**
We hold **the land, our** ships **the sea,**
 So **let the foe draw nigh** ;
The Briton's **life is** liberty;
 We must **be** free or **die** !

July 29th, 1874.

———

OUR DRAGONS OF THE DEEP.

STAND Britons by your flag, the sign
 No craven hearts are we ;
The deeds that **in our** history shine
 Repeated now must **be.**
What though our wooden walls no more
 On Neptune's **bosom sleep** ;
We've iron watchers by the shore,—
 Our Dragons of the deep.

CHORUS.

Be steady ! be steady, boys !
We're ready, aye ready, boys,
　The savage sea to sweep ;
Whoever will may dare, **boys**,
But let the world beware, **boys** !
　Our Dragons **of** the deep.

'T was not **our gallant** ships that sailed,
　With Nelson's **flag** unfurled,
That 'gainst **our** stubborn foes prevailed,
　And bravely beat the world,
But the stout hearts **of** British oak,
　That bled the land **to keep** ;
And **such are we, let none provoke**
　Our **Dragons of the deep.**

CHORUS.

Be steady ! **be** steady, boys !
We're ready, aye ready, boys,
　The savage sea to sweep ;
Whoever will may **dare, boys,**
But let the world beware, boys !
　· Our Dragons of the deep.

We love the fair white flag of peace,
　Which floats above our head ;

But rather than our rights should cease,
    We'll stain it deep with red;
The trackless sea shall be our path,
    And we to war will leap,
When we have heated with **our wrath**
    Our Dragons **of** the deep.

CHORUS.

Be steady ! **be** steady, boys !
We're **ready,** aye ready, boys,
    The **savage** sea **to** sweep;
Whoever will may dare, boys,
But let **the** world **beware, boys !**
    Our Dragons **of** the deep.

December 7th, 1872.

PALMERSTON.

OUR grand old State was labouring **in** the storm,
    And **chaos** threatened with its cloud of doom,
When the whole nation loudly cried " Reform,
    And give us one to **lead** us through the gloom."

Then at her worst, her **time of greatest need,**
    Forth stept the man o'erleaping every bar,
And threw himself upon her curbless steed,
    And rode triumphant through the thundering War.

To him the tempests on the land and sea
　　Were but as empty bubbles, light as air,
" It MUST be done," was Palmerston's decree ;
　　And Britain's praise is ringing everywhere.

Bideford, 1854.

FAITH IN HUMAN PROGRESS.

O GLORIOUS hope ! the offspring of great souls,
　　Who pass the doubters with a noble scorn ;
And he who, valiant, foul desire controls,
　　Or strives to crush it, hastens in the morn
When passion, foe of purity and light,
Shall yield to reason and the law of right.

Degrade the matter, you pollute the mind,
　　When sluggish reason idle makes the will ;
Thus, you the soul in folly's fetters bind,
　　And all the man imbruted standeth still.
Give honour to the body, base of all,
And virtue then may answer wisdom's call.

1879.

YE WARWYCKSHYRE HUNTTE.

Yᴇ huntte yₑ huntte onne Suttoune chaase !
    Yoho ! tanteevyee, tanteevyee !
Ye houndés alle offe myghte ande paace,
Ande lordes ande ladyes fayre o' faace
Doe merrye maake yᵉ mornynge.
    Yoho ! tanteevyee, tanteevyee !

Ye aunciente dogge hee gyvethe tongue,
    Yoho ! tanteevyee, tanteevyee !
Yt yˢ ye deepe-mouthede wolffe hounde's songe,
Ryde ladyes gaye ande lordes alonge,
Ande merrye maake yᵉ mornynge.
    Yoho ! tanteevyee, tanteevyee !

Ye wolffe yˢ rouzéde fro yˢ layre,
    Yoho ! tanteevyee, tanteevyee !
Presse harde yᵉ lordes ande ladyes fayre,
Ye gaame'ₛ afoote ande scenttes yᵉ ayre,
Soe merrye yᵘ yᵉ mornynge.
    Yoho ! tanteevyee, tanteevyee !

And nowe ye quarrye yˢ yᵉ boare !
    Yoho ! tanteevyee, tanteevyee !
Ye hunttesmanne bolde yˢ toe yᵉ fore,
Ye milk-whyte steede hee runnythe gore
Soe merrye yˢ yᵉ mornynge,
    Yoho ! tanteevyee, tanteevyee !

Seehoe ! seehoe ! ye hayre herr forme,
     Yoho ! tanteevyee, tanteevyee !
Shee leeveyethe doublynge lyke ye worme,
Ande cunnynge runneythe fro ye storme,
Soe merrye in ye mornynge.
     Yoho ! tanteevyee, tanteevyee !

Fro ye greene covere o' ye woode,
     Yoicks ! tallyhoe, tanteevyee !
Ye vyxene offe ye vulpyne broode
Afore ye houndes ys fleeynge shrewde
Ryghte merrye yn ye mornynge.
     Yoicks ! tallyhoe, tanteevyee !

Ande nowe yt ys ye bucke ande doe,
     Harke ! harke awaye, tanteevyee !
Ye stagge ys flyinge fro ye foe,
Ande loude ye wyndynge hornes doe blowe
Alle merrye yn ye mornynge.
     Harke ! forrwarrde, harke ! tanteevyee !

Nowe, chauntynge, lordes and dames o' Courte
     Synge sweetlye alle tanteevyee !
Forre stagge ye hunttesmanne soundeyethe morte
Longe lyve ye kynge and royalle sporte
Soe merrye ys ye mornynge.
     Yoho ! tanteevyee, tanteevyee !

V

TO THE RIGHT HONOURABLE THE EARL OF DERBY.

God strengthen thee, great Athlete in the fight.
Our Hercules who doth the dragon War
Hold in a deadly grip.   Henceforth afar
Thy name shall be the synonym of might
Armed with th' invulnerable panoply of right.
Keep thou thy place despite the baleful jar.
The hour is dark, be still our Guiding Star,
And we will follow thee into the light.
" Our greatest British interest is PEACE."
This was the clarion-note that made thy foes
From wanton vapourings for bloodshed cease,
And till the records of all time shall close,
May Heaven unto thy stock give large increase
As safeguards for the dear old land's repose.
1878.

SONG OF THE HAPPY MAN.

THE lord loves his acres, the miser his gold,
  The hunter his horse, and his hounds ;
The farmer his flock, and the warrior bold
  The charge, when the clarion sounds ;
     And the sailor his lass,
     And the beauty her glass,

And the reaper a bonny blue sky :—
    But give me a cot,
    With true love for my lot,
And a sparkle of mirth for my eye,
    And this ditty I'll sing,
    With the pride of a king,
" Though the cash in my coffer be small,
    The best of all wealth,
    Is a stock of **good** health,
With a heart that is thankful for all."

While the duke has his castle, the monarch his crown,
    The courtier his title and name,
And their ladies repose on their couches of down,
    And the hero is honour'd with fame ;
    I will journey through life,
    Without envy or strife,
Looking out for its **beautiful** flow'rs ;
    And carry a light,
    For adversity's night,
And honey to sweeten the sours ;
    And merrily sing,
    As I march with a swing,
" Since honesty feareth no fall,
    The best of all wealth,
    Is a good stock of health,
With a heart that is thankful for all."

Let the lord have his land, and the miser his gold,
  And the hunter **his** horse, and his hounds,
And the farmer his flock, and the warrior bold
  His charge, when the clarion sounds ;
      And the sailor his lass,
      And the beauty her glass,
And the reaper his bonny bright sky :—
      But with love for my lot,
      In a sweet little cot,
And a sparkle of mirth for my eye ,
      I my ditty will sing,
      Spite of Poverty's sting,
" Though the cash in my coffer be small,
      The best of all wealth,
      Is a good stock of health,
With a heart that is thankful for all."

This new volume of Mr. CAPERN's lyrics will confirm the high reputation which his previous works have deservedly obtained. His songs are peculiarly distinguished by their refinement, their freshness, and their simplicity. . . . Mr. CAPERN displays poetic genius of the highest order.—*Observer.*

One of the truest and sweetest of those nature-inspired poets to whom verse-making is a solace and recreation after the physical toils of a hard day's work.—*Morning Star.*

He sings, because his heart overflows with an intense love of nature, because the beauties and melodies of the world around him have filled his eyes and ears with their loveliness and sweetness, and his heart with ecstasy that breaks forth into song. The poet's features glow with a divine light, because he has seen nature face to face and caught the glory of her countenance.—*London Review.*

It is delightful to think that there is such a person roaming, writing, and scribbling in our land.—*Guardian.*

His ballads and songs have now become universally popular, alike charming the ears and reaching the hearts of the rich and the poor.—*Quiver.*

Mr. CAPERN **has** long been known as **a poet of no mean** order, and **the fame** he has acquired as a **sweet and natural** singer will by no means be detracted from by the *Wayside Warbles.* The lyrics contained in the volume are, like those which ha**ve** preceded them, remarkable for their sweetness and simplicity.—*City Press.*

This third volume **of** poems by Mr. EDWARD CAPERN fully bears out the judgment by which the public have assigned **to** him the rank of a genuine poet. There is no fustian about these compositions, no forced utterance, no feeling merely simulated, **and** therefore no hollow imitation of other poets. **They** are the simple, fervid outpourings of actual emotion, and **have the** sparkling freshness of their origin about them. There is something touching in the fact that these beautiful strains are the music of an humble unsophisticated heart holding communion with nature alone, and gathering its inspiration from her every-day aspects.—*Daily News.*

Here is a true poet. . . . A man who sings because **song** is his natural language. . . . Sing on Mr. CAPERN.— ***Press.***

Whoever loves a lively or a plaintive measure simply sung, and scenes that breathe of open air and open heart, will find his tone less masterful than the nightingale, but not less delightful than the lark or the linnet.—*Illustrated London News.*

Full of **warm and** simple sentiments, as refreshing as the scent of clover or new-mown grass, or the sweet honeysuckle of the beautiful Devonshire hedges and lanes.—*Morning Post.*

A genuine poet of nature, and, while he chirps about **Devonshire** and flowers and birds, is simply delicious. It is pleasant to give such unqualified praise to a self-taught songster, for such **men,** as a rule, are indifferent and impertinent versifiers. CAPERN, however, is 'real grit.'—*Fun.*

Mr. CAPERN has been deservedly praised for his hearty **love** of nature and the fresh homeliness of his language. **Mr.** CAPERN'S songs are all unaffected, and many of them **truly** graceful. There is sunshine **in** them and the fragrance **of** flowers.—*Public Opinion.*

These 'Wayside Warbles' are indeed thoroughly full of interest, not merely because of their being the effusions of a self-educated mind, but because they are full of genius, and breathe words and **sentiments** that **would do** honour to the largest intelligence that was ever employed in giving delight to our fellow men.—*Bell's Weekly Messenger.*

He was recognised long ago as a man with a real gift of song, and we are very glad to meet him again and to have an opportunity of warmly commending his book to our readers. His poems **have** about them touches **of** improvisation, which are very charming.—*Illustrated Times.*

We have **come across several pieces of a high order.—** *Athenæum.*

An excellent poet; and this his third volume is in every way worthy to rank with his previous productions.— *Workman's Advocate.*

Mr. CAPERN **has now** an established poetic **reputation.** His first volume **at** once secured it, and we are glad **to record** the progressiveness of his genius and his culture. **We** have carefully compared his first published volume with this, his third, and have sought in vain for any grace or beauty discerned in the former, which does not find representation in the latter ; while there are entirely **new** delights developed in the 'Wayside Warbles,' which were immature and only germinating in the poet's mind, when **the** volume of 'Poems' published in 1856 saw the light. He is a perfect master of melody, and as good a handicraftsman in the uses of metre, manner, and language, as any poet of the most classic epochs of the divine art.—*Atlas.*

We wish all **our** readers would read this volume of poems by EDWARD CAPERN. **He is** the Robert Burns of Devonshire, and we think that some **of** his verses equal anything the Scotch bard ever wrote in the way of touching pathos and beauty. . . While he walks, he ' warbles by the wayside ' about everything **he** sees—lads and lasses, flowers, trees, barn-yards, mills, and **rills. He** gives them the pulse and **voice** of life, and sets them **a-singing** for very joy.—*Elihu Burritt in* **the** *" Bond."*

A volume of mostly lyric poems, which have **been** frequently and favourably reviewed by the English **press.** Brought into contact with nature, and with ever-varying scenes of rural life, by his engagements, his poetic genius formed these phenomena into as many poems, which thus bear a most estimable impress **of** objective truth. And as his mind is able most fervently to embrace all the charms of nature around him, he drinks in the warm sunshine **in** full draughts, and shouts with joy at the **sight of the** endless blue heavens. Nature to him teems with **life, and birds** sing to him, he joining their chorus in praise of **Spring or the Creator.** We must confess that subjectively also he **possesses** everything that makes **the** poet. They **stand far** above the **common,** and full many may be thought **worthy of** taking a place **in our** collections of English poetry, **for which** they are eminently fitted, on account of their **ethic** and Christian spirit.—*Herrig's Archiv für Studium der neuern Sprachen und Literaturen (Herrig's Archives for the Study of Modern Languages and Literatures.*

He is evidently one of those born poets, whose sensitiveness of nature, susceptibilities to the glories of the natural world, and deep feeling for all relating to humanity, joined with a love of music, combine to form some of the most welcome authors **and true** poets of our time.—*Birmingham Journal.*

The promise which Mr. CAPERN gave in **his** first volume of poems, published in 1856, has been fulfilled. The indubitable proofs of poetic genius which that work contained, are **com**pletely confirmed by the publication of **this,** his third volume. We find in his latest works the same truthfulness to nature ; the same simplicity of language and subject ; the same musical flow of verse, compelling you to sing the poems.—*Birmingham Gazette.*

His songs have gained for him the high and not altogether unmerited praise of being called the Burns of England.—*Carlisle Journal.*

In neither of his productions do we find such disagreeable fare as diluted Byronism or Tennysonianism. . . . He is original. . . . He has genius, and genius of a high order, and fortunately for song lovers, it is essentially lyrical. . . . To the measure and character of his genius, CAPERN has no equal among the English poets of the people who have chosen the ordinary English language as their vehicle of expression. Devon ought to be proud of such a poet, and so also should England, who assuredly has produced few such song writers as EDWARD CAPERN.—*Bristol Daily Press.*

We are proud of our Devonshire Burns, his Songs have made even Devon's charms more famous, and have led many a city-pent reader to visit the scenes he paints so rapturously. Every one who peruses the 'Warbles,' will confess that he has realised his hope. The same ardent love of nature inspires his muse, and gives zest and sweetness to his ditties. 'Willow Leaves' will solace many a bereaved heart by their simple pathos, and will be prized by the admirers of CAPERN's genius, as the choicest of his lyric gems.—*Exeter and Plymouth Gazette.*

His first volume of poems, so full of genuine harmony, rural beauty, homely patriotism, and spirit-stirring enthusiasm, met with distinguished success, passing through several editions, and receiving the highest encomiums that could be pronounced upon it. This was soon after followed by a second, entitled 'Ballads and Songs,' which, as a literary production, far surpassed the earlier productions of his pen : the same fresh and simple beauty was there, but they exhibited a more cultivated imagination and a richer polish. Then succeeded the 'Devonshire Melodist,' a collection of the poet's Songs, set to music by Mr. Thomas Murby, a masterly musician, who seemed to enter into the spirit of the simple themes, and gave a new charm to the poet's telling bits of mirth and melody. Instead of sitting down and beating the home preserves of his brain for pretty thoughts, his love is to roam abroad by the hedge-row and the stream, and as he catches inspiration from the birds and flowers, he sings of their beauty and fragrance,— sometimes in music simple as the sky,—a melody drawn from a few familiar strings, the fibres of the heart ; at other times in dulcet tones, resembling the elegance of Tennyson, or the

By the same Author.

pathetic beauty of Hood. What can be more dainty and amber-bright than the lines 'To a Goldfinch'?—

> ''Tis not for thy golden wing,
> Gem of the grove,' &c., &c.

Then there is 'A Maytime Wish,' 'The Missing Star,' and others full **of** poetry and sunlight. But we need not extend our notice ; we feel sure that everyone will read this new work of Mr. CAPERN's, and appreciate its wonderful beauty.—*North Devon Journal.*

The ranks of labour **are** dignified by such men as EDWARD CAPERN. His songs will live as long as the English language continues to be spoken. Music rings from his harp as unbidden as the trill **of** the lark in the cornfield, or the gush of the nightingale in the thicket. The poets of the people have sung of the people, and have identified themselves with the surroundings of their place of abode, finding food for their fancy in the incidents of every-day life. This is one mark of true genius, and is fully exemplified in the writings of Mr. CAPERN. —*Falmouth and Penryn Times.*

By the same Author.

POEMS.

KENT AND CO.

Mr. CAPERN is a real poet, **a** man whose writings will be like a gleam of summer sunshine in every household, which they enter.—*Fraser's Magazine.*

Melodious and fresh as the skylark notes, under which many of the poems were mentally composed.—*Critic.*

Pieces of fresh rural beauty coming to us like flowering boughs out of a hedge in Spring-time.—*Leader.*

Contains many exquisitely beautiful compositions, and evinces a tone of mind whose equanimity may be envied.— *Weekly Despatch.*

'There runs throughout these poems that refined tone of thought, to the expression of which a metrical form is a necessary condition—we find rich tissues of imagery, playful fancy, plentiful invention, and above all that *translation of thought into representative circumstances* that ever characterizes the true poet—such is the distinguished excellence of Keats, Shelley, Tennyson, and Alexander Smith, in all **of whom the** true poetical constitution has been preeminently visible.—*Inquirer.*

Many of the pieces have the soul of genuine poetry in them.—*Literary Gazette.*

It is what poetry was in the sweet days of Burns and Goldsmith.—*Morning Post.*

A noble poet—I have been reading CAPERN's Poems with equal attention and delight.—*W. S. Landor.*

A man of genius of a very high order, if not the highest. A poet immeasurably superior to the Bloomfields and the other self-educated versifiers presented to the reading public during the last half century. The volume must soon be in every hand.—*Standard.*

Very genuine and very touching—a noble store **of those warm** thoughts and strains of homely patriotism **in which lie the power** of the English people.—*Examiner.*

He produces rhymes equal in **harmony to** Metastasio—who wrote in the most musical language upon earth.—*North Devon Journal.*

Fresh from the fountain **wells of nature and** feeling.—*Woolmer's Gazette.*

The liquid air seems filled with the melodies of the olden time as **we read** "May" and "June." "The Lion Flag" is an Ode **of** great merit—nothing more spirit-stirring has been written on the war.—*Civil Service Gazette.*

Mr. CAPERN is one of those few men whom God has **endowed with** that rare **gift** genius.—*Birmingham Daily Press.*

The "Reverie" seems to us one of the most beautiful poems that our day **has** produced.—*Somerset County Gazette.*

Looking at the circumstances under which these Poems were written, we must regard the volume as one of the wonders of the age.—*Weekly Times.*

BALLADS AND SONGS.

KENT AND CO.

The rhymes chime together lightly and musically, the sentiment is warm, the expression rich and truthful. We mark, indeed, an advance in Mr. CAPERN's compositions. Without being more elaborate, which would imply degeneracy, considering the author's peculiar purity,—they exhibit a finer polish, and an imagination more creative, than his former writings. Nevertheless, the merit of Mr. CAPERN as a poet lies, and always will lie, in his genuine outbursts of feeling, affection, patriotism, and especially love of nature, for the " love of love " is strong within him. Entering into an unbidden partnership (so to speak) with the thrush, the linnet, and the finch, he pipes on his oaten reed, and adds something to the meadow or woodland chorus. It is easy to show, however, that his strain is not one of monotony. There is something of Tom **Hood's** quality in an apostrophe commencing—

"Christ befriend thee, poor old man."

"The Bereaved One," " The Little Scarecrow," "Polly Lee," are examples which illustrate his versatility.—*Athenæum.*

Every bird which sings amid his breezy hills, every flower which blooms within his verdant valleys he has glorified in his songs. One feels that it is such men who help to preserve the muscles of Englishmen, and the nerve of English thought. . . Mr. CAPERN has chosen the right path, let him follow it to its end ; and as he moves along we are but too happy to receive his gifts of wayside flowers. All we need do now is to cull a few charming lyrics from the volume before us, and if our readers are disposed to forego those, and such as those, for the bare chance of droning didactics, or any other description of poetry whatever, all that we can say is, that we are contented with what is already pulsing with life, and joy, and beauty.—*Critic.*

Mr. CAPERN's songs are distinguished for their sweetness and cheerfulness. . . . . He sympathises thoroughly with country-folk, and enters into their sports, their loves, their humble hopes and fears, their difficulties and dangers.—*Leader.*

He reasons—

" Do not minor minstrels sing
Sweetly with the forest king?
So may my untutor'd lay
Swell the music of the day ;"

and it is really to the music of the day that his verses make addition.—*Examiner.*

The cottager's children, the wild flowers, the little maiden scaring the rooks from **the** corn, the shy lass waiting at the stile for her sweetheart—these are the themes he loves.   His songs are sung in the sultry hay-field, and around the cosy ingle in winter.   There is room in the world of song for CAPERN as well as Tennyson.—*Dublin University Magazine.*

How **he** burst upon the world with his casket of poetical jewels is assuredly known to all lovers of true poetry.—*The Poet's Magazine.*

Mr. CAPERN is one of those fortunate writers who gain **not** merely admirers but friends.   His whole creed, his whole teaching, his whole life may be summed **up** in one word—love. EDWARD CAPERN's songs had all the freshness of true poetic talent.   One could see that he did **not** write of birds and flowers because it was fashionable **to** do so, but because in his very heart of hearts he *loved* them.   The voice of a real joy rang through **all his** pleasant pages.   *Here* **was no** rhymer writing for effect ; here was a man who rambled every day through the green lanes of Devon, stopping every now and then **to listen to** the cheery carol of the thrush, or bending down to **pluck the** earliest primrose, and so of birds **and** primroses he **sang.**—*Sharpe's London Magazine.*

His ballads **and** songs are charming.   He is a poet of the **people.** The **robin,**

> " Which **ever in** the haunch of winter sings,"

is **not** dearer **to** the dwellers in quiet hamlets and lonely cottages than such a poet as Mr. CAPERN.—*The Plymouth Mail.*

The true spirit of poetry pervades every line.—*The Bideford Gazette.*

There is a breezy sunshiny freshness about the spirit and language of these (Ballads and Songs) that proclaim the poet's love of nature and admiration of his native country. In addition to the truthfulness of the portraiture the volume abounds with imagery of great poetic sweetness and **natural** tenderness.—*The Western Times.*

These songs are, **as** were his former ones, the natural outflowings of a true and noble heart, inspired with a love of all things beautiful.   .   .   .   .   Such a poet is a benefactor to his race, and **the** love with which the children of Devon receive the words of their native poet, show how fully they appreciate, and how dear to them is the son with which God has blessed them.—*The Birmingham Journal.*

THE DEVONSHIRE MELODIST.

BOOSEY AND SON.

Not only betokens the true poetical instinct, but exhibits a metrical knowledge to be derived from experience alone. His friends may greatly improve his position by sending him to London and making him take some of the work out of the ballad-writer's hands now prosecuting their career in the metropolis. We should select from the twelve "My Bonny Bell," "Come list, my love," and "Dorky May," as being especially fresh and charming.—*Standard.*

Deserving of extensive popularity.—*News of the World.*

The accompaniments and general arrangements of the whole by Mr. Murby evince a musician-like and masterly power which is highly creditable to that gentleman's taste and talent. He has evidently bestowed great care on his work, and deserves warm eulogy for his part of the volume. . . . Sweet as the May-dew on his (Mr. CAPERN's) native thornbloom, fresh as the night-wind in his native valleys.—*Sun.*

There is a good deal of real poetry in the verses. His thoughts are natural, touching, and expressed with simplicity and considerable elegance.—*London Illustrated News.*

This is a collection of melodies from the portfolio of that seraph of song who has wooed the muse among the hills and vales of merry Devon. Already it has had a large sale even in comparison with the books of the season. There are few song writers at present who for vigour and simplicity can stand up against EDWARD CAPERN, and in this collection there are several pieces which will rank among the best specimens of this species of composition.—*Trewman's Exeter Flying Post.*

The fame of our poet is too widely spread over the nation to need any of the common ways of puffing to make him known. What reader that loves poetry simple as nature, beautiful as the flowers of the field, warm as sunshine, has not CAPERN's poems among his choice treasures of the muses? . . . It would be strange if a poet should **not** have in the common acceptation of the phrase "music in his soul," who has a soul of music : it would not therefore be surprising to find that some of these airs to these airy songs are of the poet's own composing.— *Western Times.*

John Clare is dead, lionised, and lives in the temple of fame. . . . Here however is a truer singer than John Clare, and one whose songs are as genuine as the trill of the thrush in the thicket. His versification is as full of euphony as the trees of the forest shaken with a summer wind. To us he seems to stand alone in the world of lyrics, a living imitation of the lark in the heavens.—*Cornish Weekly News and Advertiser.*

A new volume from EDWARD CAPERN ! What a treat for the lovers of sweet song.—*West Briton and Cornwall Advertiser.*

Sings like a bird, but a bird with a soul in him athirst for divine influence, and claims for his own woodnotes an occasional 'like me' affinity with song of birds. . . . Has earned an enduring right to local fame among the scenes of which he sings. It will be well for our aftercomers, if they have not only the greatest of their fore-fathers still speaking to them all in books, but if also there shall be no pleasant nook of England in which the visitor may not find living words of one who has dwelt there, familiar in the household of its people as the native voice of its hills and streams, brightening with legends and pleasant memories all human interests, and making the very village grocer proud to be the grandson or greatgrandson of the village beauty, who was buried long ago, but is still blooming in a tender song, that all the lasses of the village know by heart. CAPERN's poems should be for all time as familiar by the Yeo, the Torridge, and the Taw, as daisies to a meadow. Mr. CAPERN, like other men, is a true poet when he expresses just as much as he actually believes and feels. How true a poet strangers perceive most readily, wherever there passes a strong human interest into his verse. . . . In the "Willow Leaves" he mourns the loss of his little daughter Milly, with a simple tenderness that must go home to every heart. . . . What a purity of tenderness **is** in the simplicity, which, in such a stanza as this, consecrates **the** simple words of household endearment.

> "We called her ' Precious,' ' Lamb,' and **' Sweet,'**
> And ' Pretty Cheek,' ' Pet,' ' Lily,' ' Dove :'
> Such names as mothers use above,
> When they their missing infants greet."

—*London Examiner.*